Billionaire Romance

The Billionaire and the Babysitter

Simone Carter

© Copyright 2016 Simone Carter

All rights Reserved.

ISBN-13: 978-1533447654

ISBN-10: 1533447659

Table of Contents

Prologue 6
Chapter 1: Living the Dream 11
Chapter 2: The Playboy 17
Chapter 3: A Different Side 21
Chapter 4: What Now? 26
Chapter 5: Getting Closer 33
Chapter 6: Unwelcome Guests 37
Chapter 7: The First Touch 42
Chapter 8: Uncontrollable Desires 47
Chapter 9: In Deep 53
Chapter 10: A Changed Man 59
Chapter 11: Innocence Meets Experience 65
Chapter 12: All The Way 71
Chapter 13: The Morning After 77
Chapter 14: Old Debts 84
Chapter 15: Getting On With It 91
Chapter 16: Saying Goodbye 97
Chapter 17: Trouble Is Coming 102
Chapter 18: Evil Comes Out 107
Chapter 19: Stepping Up 113
Chapter 20: Taking Care Of Business 119
Chapter 21: Much Needed Rest 124
Chapter 22: The Next Fix 131
Chapter 23: The Biggest Gamble of Them All? 138
Epilogue 140
About The Author 145
Other titles by Simone Carter 146

Prologue

Jake

I'm a gambler, a professional poker player...and damn good at what I do. Good enough to have made millions at the tables. Since I made smart investments with my money I'm now what people call filthy rich. And I make the most of it.

Most pro players have a nickname and I'm no exception. They call me the Playboy. I guess I earned the title honestly. I enjoy the fruits of my labors to the fullest and take advantage of all the doors it opens for me. It just happens that a lot of those doors go into bedrooms.

I'm not bragging when I say women are always throwing themselves at me. I'm just telling it like it is. Women tell me I'm good looking, and I guess I am. I'm 36 years old; I work out a lot and keep fit, and still have a head full of thick black hair. But I know what all those females really like is the fact I'm rich. And you'd be surprised what women will do to get to the money.

I travel extensively, both for business and pleasure. It isn't unusual to see me with a beautiful woman at my side. Of course, it's always a different woman. I'm not about to get tied down. I'm having way too much fun for that. Too many women, not enough time. I'm not fool enough to turn down what's presented to me freely. I admit, though, I'm picky about which women I choose to be with. I select women like some men select cars...I like 'em sleek, hot, and fast.

Right now I'm enjoying the company of just such a woman. Her name is Brandy and she's gorgeous. Reed slender but with full, round artificially enhanced boobs and an exotic face framed by cascades of lush, silky dark hair. She shows off her assets well, the plunging top of her scarlet halter providing a free preview of coming attractions. A scintillating scent of musk surrounds her and her moist, full lips would entice any man with an ounce of testosterone in him. I'd let her maneuver me to a secluded area on the balcony of my Las Vegas penthouse and am fully prepared to be seduced. I'm horny, she's available. The perfect combination.

My hands are full of her silicone rich breasts when the phone rings. My first inclination is to ignore it. Whatever it is can wait until I quench my lust. My dick was so hard I could pound nails with it. I just wanted to fuck this woman...now.

The phone stopped ringing, then immediately started again. Damn. What was so fucking important that it couldn't wait another 30 minutes? I reach for my phone to turn it off but before I push the button I note the phone number. The area code is 219. Michigan City, Indiana. That had to be family.

I don't actually have much family. Just a half-brother that's 8 years younger than me. We'd never really been close but we were all each other had. Our mom was dead, neither one of us had ever known our dads, and I'd always tried to be there for Danny.

That hadn't been easy. Right after high school I joined the navy. I knew it was the only way I'd ever be able to afford college. It meant leaving Danny and my mother for a while, but in the long run, they'd be better off when I had my college education. I'd be a lot better prepared to support them.

When I started winning at the tables I knew I wanted to parlay my earnings into solid income, so I started investing. One of my first investments was in my kid brother.

It was a risky venture. Me and Danny grew up in a bad part of Chicago. Gang-infested public housing. Mama working all the time. I didn't want any part of the gangsta lifestyle, though. I focused on making a better life for me, Mama, and Danny and I was smart enough to know I wouldn't find it in the hood. It wasn't easy. Sometimes it took my fists to convince certain undesirables I wasn't interested in their way of life, but I managed to stay clean. For Mama and Danny.

I did well in the Navy. Even became a SEAL. That all came to a screeching halt, though, the day I fought an IED and lost. That was the end of my military career. I started playing poker online while I was laid up recuperating and learning to walk again. Turned out I had a real knack for the game. I earned my way into a big poker tournament and won it. It took off from there. Now I'm a billionaire.

But Danny was my first investment. He was 18 when Mama died, the innocent victim of a drive by shooting while she was walking home from her night job tending bar. Danny managed to graduate high school, barely, but I knew he was getting tangled up in gangland and headed straight down a path to self-destruction.

I admit it. I bribed him to give it up. I asked him what, if anything, he loved doing, something he was passionate about. I gotta say, it blew my mind when he said cooking. I had no idea he dreamt of being a chef.

I promised him the world. I vowed to pay his way through top culinary schools, to open up a restaurant for him, to support him all the way. There was only one condition. He had to leave Chicago, get away from the gangs, away from the old crowd.

I was like a proud papa when he excelled in his schooling. I even sent him to Paris for more training. Then I asked him where he wanted his restaurant. It could be anywhere; France, Las Vegas, a tropical island. I couldn't believe it when he told me Michigan City, Indiana, just an hour outside Chicago. Why there, I asked him. Well, it turned out he'd met a girl. Eve. He wanted to get married, settle down, and that's where she lived. I said okay, fine. As long as he was happy, I was happy.

Danny worked long hours and it wasn't unusual for him to call me late at night. I didn't hear from him too often and when he called it was usually for something important. Funny, though, this call wasn't from his home phone or his cell. It wasn't from the restaurant, either.

I can't help it. My curiosity wins out over my lust. It should only take a second to tell Danny I'd call him back in an hour. That would give me time to take care of me and Miss Brandy.

But when I answered that call life as I knew it shattered like a crystal goblet dropped on a concrete floor.

Chapter 1: Living the Dream

Jenna

As usual, I woke up early enough to steal a few minutes to myself before the business of the day started. I made a cup of coffee and carried it out on the deck with me. It was the first day of June and it looked like the world was celebrating. The sunrise painted the east and the vast beauty of Lake Michigan danced before me.

I enjoy these quiet moments in the morning before the kids wake up. I'm a nanny so quiet times aren't too frequent, not with almost 4-year-old DJ and 18-month-old Lily around. Don't get me wrong. They're adorable children and I love them. They're just busy, busy, busy.

Their parents, Dan and Eve DeMarco, are always busy, too. They own a popular, trendy restaurant in Michigan City and people frequently come from as far as Chicago to eat there. Dan has his fingers in some other financial pies, too, I guess, because he certainly seems to be doing well. They're a young, beautiful couple who like the finer things in life. This house, for instance, is a showplace. Located in Long Beach, the home has magnificent lake views and beach access. The furnishings are contemporary and elegant, the color scheme predominantly white and black, with a slap of scarlet here and there.

To me it feels a bit cold and sterile but, hey, that's just me. There's nothing much fancy about me. I'm a simple girl who grew up on a farm and slopped hogs before breakfast. I'm not big into fashion. Unlike Eve, the clothes horse, you'll usually find me in jeans and a T-shirt. I typically keep my unruly rusty red curls in a pony-tail. I'm too curvy to be considered a model beauty and I don't care. Yeah, maybe I could stand to lose a couple pounds, but I'm healthy, I'm happy, and that's all that counts. Other people's opinions of my looks don't concern me.

Someday I'm going to be a lawyer. I already have a bachelor's degree in criminal justice but right now I'm taking a couple years off to save up enough money to pay for law school and this job is perfect. It pays well and room and board is included so I can stash my cash. The kids are great, living right on the lake is awesome, and Danny and Eve are easy to work for. They're gone a lot so frequently it's just me and the little ones at home. We spend a lot of time on the beach together or playing in the back yard. We take long walks, read stories, and sing songs. And just think, on top of my salary, I get rewarded with a fortune in snuggles and kisses. Yeah, I really do like my job.

Speaking of which, I need to get the day started. Lily, the early riser, would be awake any minute needing her diaper changed and some good morning cuddles.

I got the kids up and dressed and fed, stopped DJ from emptying the entire container of fish food into the aquarium, and saved Lily from crashing into the glass coffee table when she lost control of her eager toddling footsteps. We made a quick trip into town for Storytime at the library where my friend Frankie, aka Francesca, worked and got home in time for the kids to have lunch with their just out of bed parents.

This is the time of day the kids most often see their parents, before Dan and Eve get their busy schedules going. Soon they'll be off to take care of things at the restaurant, go to a meeting or shopping, or on some other quest. I don't know how they do it. They are always on the go. If those were my two adorable children, I'd want to spend a lot more time with them, but, again that's just me. I guess we all have different goals in life.

By evening the kids and I are tired. I make them a quick dinner of chicken patties and sweet potato fries. It's one of their favorites. Little do they know I hide pureed cauliflower in the chicken breading. It's one of the tricks I've learned for getting them to eat more veggies.

Lily barely stays awake long enough to take a bath. By the time I slip her pink jammies on her little body she's nodding in my arms. I slide her in to her crib, turn the baby monitor on, and go back to DJ.

Being the big boy he is, DJ stays awake longer than his baby sister. I notice he seems a bit quieter than usual though and when he comes to crawl in my lap I think he feels a bit warm. I drop a gentle kiss on his forehead as he snuggles against me. Yep, definitely warm. This calls for a dose of children's Tylenol before bed.

I get DJ tucked in clutching his old, worn lop-eared rabbit and go to my own room. It's a small room but it has an attached bath and a door onto the balcony overlooking the lake. Not bad for a glorified babysitter's quarters.

I climb into bed with a new mystery novel and find myself quickly caught up in the intriguing plot. After a while, though, I can't keep my eyes open and reluctantly lay the book aside. I fall asleep almost instantly.

It feels like only moments pass when the sound of crying wakes me. Damn, I'd been in the middle of a great dream, too. Blearily I look at the clock. Three in the morning.

I hear the cry again and stumble down the hallway. The sound is coming from DJ's room. Yep, there he is, out of bed and kneeling on his window seat, his little hands pressed against the pane of glass.

"DJ, sweetness, what's wrong?" I sit down next to him and pull him into my arms.

"My tummy hurts," he hiccups.

"Aw, is that what woke you up?" I run my hand over his forehead. It felt cooler now than when I tucked him in be. "Do you feel sick?"

He shakes his head but tears continue to roll down his cheeks.

"Mommy and Daddy."

"Yes, honey, they'll be home soon."

"They outside." He pointed a pudgy finger towards the window. "They fall down."

"Oh, honey, you must have had a bad dream." I gently rub his back, trying to soothe him.

"No, no, no. They outside. They fall down. I saw them." His lip protruded as he shook his head vigorously. "Look."

"Okay, let's look." I agree just to pacify him and get on my knees to peer out the window beside him. "Now, see…" I broke off when I saw the car in the driveway. The headlights were on, the doors open. A figure lay on the ground, not moving. What the hell?

"DJ, you stay here. I'm going to go check."

"I wanna go, Jenna. Take me."

"No, buddy, you stay here. I mean it. You watch me out the window."

Pausing only to grab my robe to throw over my nightshirt and slip my feet into flip flops, I scurried down the stairs, my heart thumping like crazy. I couldn't imagine any good reason for the scene I just viewed. This could be bad, very bad. I was terrified to look.

"Come on, Jenna, put on your big girl panties and go see what's wrong." I spoke the words out loud to bolster my flagging courage, and then, to give it another boost, I grab a knife as I pass through the kitchen to slip out the side door.

I hesitate on the porch steps; the only sound is the blood swooshing through my veins like the echo of nearby Lake Michigan pounding on the shore. Slowly, I take a step, then another. The glare of the headlights momentarily blind me as I round the corner.

Then I'm there, just a few feet away from the lifeless form on the drive. It's Dan DeMarco. Blood paints the front of his once white shirt, a dribble of scarlet trickling from his mouth.

Oh, God, I want to scream, I want to freak out. For a minute I feel the world tilt drunkenly, swirling in a gray fog. Somehow I manage to pull it together a little bit and realize I need to find Eve.

All I did was walk around the car. There she was, face down, as if she'd been trying to run away. One of her black stilettos lay on its side a few feet behind her, like Cinderella's glass slipper abandoned at the ball.

But this sure in the hell was no fucking fairy tale.

Chapter 2: The Playboy

Jake

My private jet was in the air headed for Indiana an hour after I received the call but it still felt like the trip took forever. I guess I was in shock because time seemed to move in slow motion. Danny and Eve, both gone. I couldn't fathom it.

By the time I got to the house the sun had been up for a few hours. The sky was crystal clear, bluer than the lake shimmering in the distance. Even at this early hour I needed my sunglasses. It didn't seem right. The world should be dim and gray, raining, tears pouring from the sky, mourning the loss of my brother and his wife.

I had to get clearance to enter the house. I waited restlessly until I was finally permitted to go inside. I wanted to see my niece and nephew with my own eyes, make sure they were okay.

When the cop escorted me into the living room my eyes immediately landed on the curvy redhead holding my niece. This must be the nanny Dan had mentioned. Even at a tense moment like this I couldn't help but notice her voluptuous figure clad in a short pink terry cloth robe, her riotous red curls tumbling around her shoulders. Her legs, her long, long, legs, were exposed. Lily clung to her, her pudgy little arms wrapped around the woman's neck, the baby's soft black waves nestled by her chin, a stark contrast to the woman's pearly white skin. DJ stood next to her, glued to her side, sticking to her like he would never let her go.

For a long moment my gaze and hers collided. I studied her fresh face, her youthfulness. She looked too young to be responsible for the care of the two children, yet obviously they trusted her. They both anchored themselves to her like she was the only safe port in the storm of activity taking place around them.

DJ's face lit up, however, when he recognized me.

"Uncle Jake!" He ran towards me, his arms outstretched, and I swung him up in the air. "Uncle Jake, Mommy and Daddy fell down."

"I heard that, buddy. That's why I'm here." I closed my eyes against the ache that pierced through me, holding his sturdy little body close, my big hand cupping his head. "I'm here, buddy. I'm here to stay and take care of you."

I didn't fail to see the sudden flare of concern in the babysitter's eyes. Their color deepened to almost purple, and a faint rosy tint bloomed across her cheekbones. So, she didn't like that idea. Well, too bad. These kids were my family, my only niece and nephew. And now they were my responsibility. I knew Danny had a will and that I had been named both executor and guardian for the children.

I also knew I would need help. Since the kids already knew her I would like her to stay on but only if she respected the fact that she was the nanny. I am the guardian so my word goes.

She broke her silence.

"Mr. DeMarco. I can't tell you how sorry I am." Her eyes welled and I could tell by their redness this wasn't the first time today she'd fought tears. "It's...unbelievable..." her voice trailed off and she blinked rapidly managing to stop the impending waterworks, thank goodness. Then I saw her visibly straighten her shoulders and steel her spine, her chin tilting upwards.

"I was just going to fix the kids some breakfast. I promised them blueberry pancakes. Would you like some?"

"Sure. I'll be there in a bit. First I want to talk to the lead detective."

"And I want to talk to you, too, Mr. DeMarco. I'm Detective Marcus Wayne." The guy that spoke looked more like a defensive end then a police officer. He was as tall as me, but heavier, built like an ox. I guess some would call him handsome if they liked the macho jock type.

"I'll see you in the kitchen." The redhead herded the kids out of the room. I think I remembered Danny telling me her name was Jenna.

"Sorry we have to meet under these circumstances." Wayne said, offering his hand. "This has got to be a shock."

"That's an understatement." I ran my hand across my tension tight neck. "Tell me what you know."

I paced as Wayne talked. He painted an ugly picture.

"Apparently Mr. and Mrs. DeMarco had just pulled into the driveway. They were ambushed. Both died from gunshots. Jenna Jordan, the nanny, found them and called it in."

God, no wonder the woman had looked so pale. It must have been traumatic as hell to discover Danny and Eve gunned down like that.

"So tell me, Mr. DeMarco, do you know of anyone who would want your brother and his wife dead?"

Chapter 3: A Different Side

Jenna

My hands shook as I stirred the pancake batter. I'd plopped Lily into her high chair and given her a banana to chew on while I worked. DJ sat in his booster seat running a Hot Wheels car across the table in front of him, soft motor noises emitting from his throat. They were both feeling much calmer than I was.

My stomach still churned even though I'd already thrown up twice. I wanted to scream hysterically, to cry my heart out, but I had to stay calm for the kids. I had to keep my mind focused on these babies, these tiny people I had come to love. I couldn't lose it now.

The coffee was brewing and I poured myself a cup as the pancakes cooked on the griddle.

"I could use a cup of that, too."

I spun around at the sound of the deep voice. Jake DeMarco had entered the room silently as I was lost in my thoughts. Caught there in his gaze I was suddenly very aware I still wore only my short robe over my even shorter nightshirt. I felt color begin to creep from my neck upwards. Damn. The curse of a redhead. I could never hide embarrassment.

Silently I grabbed another cup and poured the steaming brew into it. When I handed it to him our hands brushed and I jerked as if I'd been zapped by an electric shock. *What the hell?*

I spun away from him, turning back to the griddle and fumbling as I started flipping pancakes. What did you say to someone who had just lost their brother and sister-in-law? Especially someone like Jake DeMarco, a man who Danny idolized, a self-made billionaire, *the Playboy*.

"Why don't you sit down? These pancakes are just about done."

He didn't answer, just took a seat next to DJ.

"Hey, buddy, what you got there? Cool. A '57 Chevy."

For the next couple minutes, I busied myself with the pancakes and Jake and DJ chattered away about cars. Lily, oblivious to the trauma surrounding them, babbled happily as she gnawed at the banana dissolving in her hand.

I fixed each of the kids a plate and slid a stack of pancakes in front of Jake. I hustled around, cutting up the pancakes for the kids and refilling sippy cups with milk. Finally, I sank onto a chair and began to feed Lily bites of golden pancakes enhanced by a generous amount of fresh blueberries.

"Here you go, honeybunch, take a bite." I guided the spoon into Lily's eager open mouth.

"So DJ." The softness in Jake's voice surprised me. He didn't seem like a man with anything soft about him. "You saw your mommy and daddy fall down."

My breath caught in my throat.

DJ's big brown eyes grew wide. "Mommy and Daddy fall down. They didn't get up." The little boy's lower lip trembled and I felt my heart break all over again. "I hollered at them. Get up! But they didn't get up."

"Did you see anything else, buddy? Did you see any other people?"

The silence in the room was deafening. Finally, DJ answered.

"I saw a man point at Mommy and Daddy. A man chased Mommy." A frown crossed DJ's little face as he drew his brows together as he tried to remember. "They fall down."

My eyes shot to meet Jake's. DJ had seen more than I realized. Lord help us, this three year old child was the eyewitness to the murder of his parents.

Jake

I watched Jenna as a look of shock, then realization, swept across her face before she managed to regain a calm expression. I noticed her hand shook as she scooped the next bite into Lily's mouth.

"DJ, you met Detective Wayne, right?" I smiled at my nephew. "He's a nice guy. He's going to help us find who made Daddy and Mommy fall down. He wants to talk to you when you get done eating, okay?"

"Will you be with me, Uncle Jake? And Jenna, too?" His brow furrowed seriously, a wary look in his eyes.

"Sure we will, buddy. Right, Jenna?"

"If that's what you want, DJ, of course we will." Her voice sounded reassuring for DJ's sake, but concern filled her eyes. I understood. I, too, wanted to protect this little boy who looked so much like my brother.

"Great. Now eat a bit more and drink your milk. You must have been drinking a lot of milk lately; you've grown so much since I saw you at Christmas."

"Yep, I drink my milk. Daddy says it what gives me muscles." He held up a scrawny arm to show off his skinny bicep.

"Wow, will you look at those muscles pop." I reached out and squeezed his little arm, letting loose an admiring whistle. "Impressive."

"Daddy says someday they'll be bigger than his."

I studied his sweet, innocent features while faking a smile and nodding agreeably. For a moment grief nearly overwhelmed me. Danny wouldn't be here to watch DJ's muscles grow, or to see him go to school, or to watch him play Little League. Danny wouldn't watch Lily graduate or walk her down the aisle. Danny and Eve would never hold their grandchildren.

Then when I was just about choking on the grief another emotion took over. Anger. Fiery, bitter anger. The heat mounted in me, building from a smoldering spark deep inside my gut to an all-consuming flame, engulfing me in a burning fire, igniting a determination to find the devil that stole those special times from my niece and nephew, stole the future from my brother and sister-in-law.

At that moment I swore a vow to myself and to Danny. If it took every last cent I had, I would make that bastard pay.

Chapter 4: What Now?

Jenna

It seemed the day would never end. Police were everywhere, swarming all over the yard and the house. Normally we would have been asked to leave the home since it was now a crime scene, but because the actual murders took place outside we were allowed to remain as long as we stayed indoors and no one besides police was allowed entry.

Of course, cops were still everywhere, searching the house, confiscating computers, cell phones, and papers of all kinds. Anything that might give them a clue as to who committed this horrible act.

I was exhausted. I hadn't slept much the night before and shock and grief weighed me down. After breakfast I managed to change into jeans and a T-shirt and put Lily down for her nap before joining Jake, DJ, and Detective Wayne in the study. DJ clutched his scruffy rabbit and sat on the sofa between me and his uncle. His thumb was stuck in his mouth and his eyes were wide as he eyed Detective Wayne sitting in a chair nearby. Wayne looked almost as uncomfortable as DJ. I guess that was understandable. He probably didn't have to interview an eyewitness to a murder who happened to be just three and a half years old very often.

"So, DJ, what woke you up last night?"

DJ fingered the rabbit's ear and cast his eyes towards the floor.

"Did you hear a noise or something?" Wayne tried to speak softly but his voice was naturally gruff. DJ leaned against me and hid his face in my side. I slipped my arm around him and stroked his silky curls.

"DJ, remember when I came in your room last night? When you were looking out the window?" He nodded silently, his face still buried in my ribcage. "I came because I heard you. What made you wake up and start crying? Do you remember?"

"My tummy hurt." He spoke so low he was barely audible.

"Yes. Your tummy hurt. So what made you go look out the window?"

"I heard a noise. It was a car."

"And you wanted to see the car."

His little head bobbed affirmatively.

Detective Wayne tried again to get DJ to talk to him.

"Then what happened, DJ?"

"I saw Daddy's car."

"You're doing a good job, DJ. Tell me what you saw next."

DJ stuck his thumb back in his mouth and blinked furiously.

"Will you tell me what happened next?" Jake took hold of DJ's little hand and the little boy looked directly into his eyes. "I really want to hear about it."

"A man jumped out of the bushes. Daddy opened the car door and got out. They talked. Then the man pointed at Daddy and he fell down." DJ's fingers worried the rabbit's ear as he told his uncle what he'd seen. Tears welled in his eyes. "Daddy didn't get up."

Jake reached out and pulled his nephew close to him, his eyes closing to cover his pain.

"What happened then, buddy?"

"Mommy got out of the car and started to run away. The man pointed at Mommy and she fell down, too." He lifted both palms and shrugged his shoulders.

"What did the man do then, DJ?" Wayne asked the next question.

"He runned away."

"Did you see where he ran to? Did he get in a car?" Wayne was leaning forward, his hands on his knees.

"I don't know where he went. He just runned away."

"Can you tell us what the man looked like, DJ?"

DJ just sat there looking confused. Wayne rubbed his hands together before folding them beneath his chin. Questioning children wasn't his forte.

"Was it a big man, DJ? As big as Uncle Jake?" I couldn't stop my gaze from raking over the muscular man sitting on the other side of the little boy.

"Not that big." DJ said emphatically.

"Was he more like Daddy sized?"

DJ nodded his head.

"Could you see his hair, DJ?" Jake tossed out the question.

"He didn't have no hair."

"You mean he was bald?" Wayne fired the question at the little boy.

DJ gave the man a look like he was stupid.

"I mean he didn't have no hair."

Wayne tried again to ask more questions but it soon became obvious DJ had had enough. He began kicking his feet against the couch and carrying on a conversation with his rabbit. Finally, he leaned against me and sighed.

"I'm tired, Jenna."

Jake straightened up and gave Wayne a stern eye. "Then I think that's enough for now. You want me to tuck you in for a nap, buddy?"

DJ didn't speak, just held his arms up for his uncle to take him. Without another word Jake strode out of the room carrying his nephew.

Now the endless day was finally drawing to a close. The police had left and I just finished tucking the kids into bed. I stepped out of DJ's room and softly closed the door jerking sharply when Jake came unexpectedly around the corner.

"Kids settled in?"

I nodded, unable to find my voice in his company. There was something intimidating about this man. I'm not a petite woman by any means but for some reason I feel smaller, more vulnerable in his presence.

"Then let's have a beer and talk." It wasn't a question. It sounded more like an order. I would normally have bristled at such a commanding tone but I was just too tired to argue with him. Besides, a beer sounds pretty good right about now. My nerves could use it.

We walk silently to the kitchen and I take two longnecks from the fridge. I popped off the caps, handed him one, and sank onto a stool at the kitchen island. Neither of us spoke, just took a long guzzle from our bottles.

After a few moments he broke the silence.

"I want to thank you for being so good with the kids. I can tell they love you."

I took another swig before answering, my eyes on the bottle in my hand.

"I love them, too."

"I'm going to need help taking care of them. I don't know much about kids. Are you willing to stay on?" He turned the full power of his dark chocolate gaze on me and a tremor ran down my spine.

A part of me screamed that I should run away. Get as far away from this murder scene...and this man...as fast as possible. I didn't need the drama of another murder. This was hitting way too close to home. My own parents had been murdered during a home invasion just two years ago. I couldn't handle going through this again.

Besides, there's this weird thing going on with Jake. Something about him. Something disturbing, almost frightening. I feel a strange power emanating from him. A power that threatens my independence, that makes me feel weak. Somehow I know he's dangerous. Dangerous to my sanity, hazardous to my heart. Call it instinct or whatever.

But then I thought about those babies whose whole lives had been turned upside down. Those poor little ones who were orphans now. They had nobody but their Uncle Jake, a man who flew in and out of their lives a few times a year. Plus, there was Aunt Tarina, Eve's irresponsible younger sister who'd recently gotten out of drug rehab. Not one to count on.

Jake doesn't know DJ likes his back scratched when he's falling asleep. He doesn't know Lily loves to be rocked and sung to. I am the only remaining familiar person in their lives. Could I really walk away and leave them?

I didn't speak, couldn't speak. I sat there biting my lower lip and swirling the beer bottle in little circles on the counter...

"Please. Say you'll stay. The kids need you." He drew in a long breath before adding in a soft voice, "I need you."

Chapter 5: Getting Closer

Jake

Nobody's ever called me a coward. There's not much that scares me. But right now, I'll admit it, I'm terrified. What the hell do I know about taking care of two toddlers? I don't know how to change diapers, or what to feed them, or what to do if they get sick. I may know a lot about a lot of things but I don't know anything about kids. I couldn't do this on my own. I tried not to let my panic show but I was about to choke on it.

I couldn't tell by looking at her if Jenna was going to say yes or no. She wouldn't look at me, her gaze fastened on the beer bottle. Her skin was pale, her shoulders slumped. Poor kid. She'd had a rough day.

But so had I. And if she refused to stay on, it was about to become rougher.

Finally, I couldn't take it anymore. I reached out and pulled her face around, forcing her to look me in the eyes.

"I'll double your salary."

A light flared in her eyes and at first I thought it was greed. Then, when those full pink lips stiffened into a straight line and her chin reared up, I realized it was anger.

"Look, Mr. DeMarco..."

"I told you to call me Jake."

"Fine, then. Mr. DeMarco, Jake...*the Playboy*." Her voice was low and scornful. "If I decide to stay, it won't be because you bought me. The only reason I'm even considering staying is because of those kids. Your money has nothing to do with it."

The headache I'd been fighting all day pounded louder in my skull. Wearily I ran a hand over my eyes.

"Are you telling me you're worried about my reputation?"

"Well living here alone with just you and the kids won't do much for mine." She practically rolled her eyes. "And you are known to be a ladies' man."

"Are you afraid I'll seduce you?" I had to admit, I wouldn't mind tangling with this fiery red head. Sure, she wasn't my usual type, but I have to say there is something tantalizing about her, something that arouses my male interest.

"Certainly not."

I enjoyed watching the blush bring bright color to her cheeks. Her backbone became ramrod straight and her eyes flashed purple lightning.

"Oh, I know I'm not your type. I'm not a size two bimbo with fake boobs. But you might get bored here in sedate little Michigan City and decide to try to hit what's handy. I want it known up front I am not interested."

Part of me was amused by her defiant stance and part of me was offended by her vehemence. Was the thought of bedding me so horrible?

But I needed Jenna to stay. I would be helpless when it came to handling the kids.

"I promise not to molest you. Does that make you feel better?"

For a long moment she didn't say a word, just began picking at the label on her beer bottle. You could see a conflict of emotions playing across her face but finally she heaved a deep sigh and turned to face me."

"I'll stay for the kids."

I didn't realize I'd been holding my breath until it whooshed out of me.

"Thank you, Jenna. I mean that. You don't know how scared I was you'd say no."

Jenna

I really didn't have a choice. I couldn't walk away from DJ and Lily now. I just hoped the hell it wasn't a mistake. Jake DeMarco wasn't a man you could ignore. His mere presence in a room commanded attention. I understood why he'd earned his nickname. A man who looked like that even without money would be hard for almost any woman to resist.

But not me. I wasn't in the market for a fling. I refused to be used by a man who went through women like toilet paper then flushed them away. No, I was here strictly for those babies.

"So we're clear on the ground rules then?" I looked him straight in the eyes.

"Absolutely. Hands off the babysitter." He raised his hands in the air and returned my eye contact.

"Okay then." I hopped off the stool and tossed my bottle in the trash. "I'm going to check on the kids and go to bed."

I drew my pride around me and walked out of the room. Well, that was awkward. But I had to make sure he understood where I drew the line. I wasn't one of the playboy's little playmates.

I looked in on both children, stopping to pull the blanket up over Lily, her little rump sticking in the air, and picked up DJ's rabbit from where it had fallen to the floor and tucked it in beside him. God, they look so innocent, so vulnerable. Their whole future had changed in a moment today. Tears burn my eyes as I stumble into my room and collapse on my bed.

This was a nightmare. Who killed Danny and Eve? Why? Unanswered questions swirled through my head like fish caught in a whirlpool.

I dragged myself up and headed into the shower. The hot, streaming water eased the ache in my tense muscles, but it didn't do a thing for the ache in my heart.

I dried my hair, slid into a T-shirt and boxer shorts and crawled into bed. I tried to sleep but every time I closed my eyes there it was again. The image of Dan and Eve DeMarco sprawled on the ground, blood pooling around them. When I finally did drift into a restless slumber it was disturbed by terrifying dreams filled with DJ's cries and men pointing at people. They all fell down.

Chapter 6: Unwelcome Guests

Jake

The next few days would always remain a blur in my mind. There was so much to do, so many details to take care of. I stayed in touch with the police, impatient to hear they'd caught the devil that killed my brother and his wife. I began planning a double funeral even though the coroner hadn't released the bodies yet. And the phones never stopped ringing. My cell phone, the house phone here at Danny's, even Jenna's cell phone rang constantly.

Some of the callers were reporters, panting for a story. Others were friends, neighbors, business associates, and employees from the restaurant. Worst of all were the calls from Eve's family. Although her parents had both passed in recent years she had a little sister, Tarina, who couldn't stop crying every time I spoke with her. She was only 24, worked as a hostess at the restaurant, and was now apparently alone in the world except for an ancient uncle and aunt.

Danny's car had been towed away by police and yellow crime scene tape still draped the property. We weren't allowed to go in and out for two days, cops crawling all over the grounds and through the house.

I thanked God hourly that Jenna had decided to stay on. She was the only calm spot in the storm. She fielded phone calls and kept the kids fed and happy. It was her that rocked and sang to Lily when the baby cried for her mamma. Jenna got up in the middle of the night when DJ woke crying from his nightmares. I heard him scream last night and raced to his room as quickly as I could but she'd beat me there. I watched from the doorway as she pulled the little boy close and kissed the top of his head, uttering soothing nonsensical words.

I couldn't help but think what a beautiful sight she made, moonlight splashing across her fiery curls. The silken locks tumbled in wild disarray halfway down her back, a sharp contrast to the short white nightie clinging to her generous curves and exposing her long golden legs nearly to her hips. I had to bite back my urge to groan when I felt my dick harden at the scene before me.

I turned away before she had a chance to see me. I had a feeling if she caught me standing there clad in just my boxers with an obvious hard on she would run like a scared rabbit. I couldn't afford to lose her now.

I'd always heard the first 48 hours after a murder are the most crucial to solving the crime and that time was now expired by nearly 24 hours. Unfortunately, according to Detective Wayne, there were still no solid leads and they were no closer to finding the killer. The frustration ate at me like a gnawing rat. I wasn't used to standing idly by when action was required. I needed to do something.

That's when I decided to bring in my own investigator. Grant Golding was the head of security for all my enterprises and he was one of the best. He better be. I paid him damn well for his services.

As soon as our 'quarantine' was lifted and we were allowed visitors I had Grant fly in and come to the house. He sat up his headquarters in Danny's old den and slept in a spare bedroom so he could work the case as much as possible. Within hours of arriving he began interviewing employees, doing background searches on any bald men who had a relationship with Danny and Eve, and gleaning as much info from the police as possible.

Tonight Jenna fixed a delicious spaghetti dinner for us then while she was putting the kids to bed Grant and I sat at the table talking and drinking beer. He brought me up to date on all he'd learned so far.

"Well, the first thing I have to say is it's a damn shame bald heads are so in style right now. You'd be amazed how many men who shave their head are amongst Danny's contacts." Grant leaned back in his chair and flashed a grin. "There are at least six that I know of already. A couple of suppliers, three employees at the restaurant, including his manager Joe Fielder, and a friend of his named Reno."

That name made my head snap up. "Reno Vasquez?"

"That's him."

I knew that name. Reno Vasquez was Danny's best childhood friend from the hood. He'd gotten caught up in the gangster lifestyle and the last I knew he was in prison for dealing drugs.

"I didn't know he'd been coming around."

"He's been at the restaurant numerous times, I guess. They say Danny always treated him as a special guest."

A block of ice molded in my stomach. Reno Vasquez. He was capable of murder. I knew it.

"What else?"

Grant glanced up as Jenna returned to the room and began to tidy up the kitchen. I couldn't help noticing the admiring glance he trailed up and down her curvaceous figure. Instantly I felt annoyed. Grant was a good looking guy and his reputation for playing the ladies was even worse than mine. A flare of protectiveness fired up within me. Huh. I wasn't usually the jealous type but if I had to name the emotion surging through me, I guess it would be called jealousy. I shook my head. I had no idea why I felt possessive of the babysitter.

"Take a close look at Reno." I spoke brusquely, shoving aside those weird feelings roiling within me. "Find out if he's got an alibi for that night."

The ringing of the landline phone shrilled and Jenna turned to grab the phone on the counter.

"DeMarco residence."

Jenna's eyes widened, her mouth fell open in shock. Her hand covered her mouth before her fingers fumbled for the speaker button so we could all hear.

"There are rumors the little boy witnessed the murders. Is that true?"

Whoa. That information had not been released to the public. How did this guy know that?

I jumped up and grabbed the phone as though I could reach in and pull the guy through it but I caught myself before I exploded. This wasn't news I wanted reported.

"Look, buddy, I don't know who you are but back off. Leave this family alone to grieve and don't be dragging three year olds into this." I grabbed the phone from Jenna's hand and hung up on the ass hat.

Chapter 7: The First Touch

Jenna

I was shaking with fury by the time Jake took the phone from me. The idea that someone would publish that information, would endanger that little boy's life, incensed me.

Jake pushed the button to disconnect the call and our gazes crashed. He looked mad as hell and I probably looked sick to my stomach. A tremor ran down my back.

"Oh, God, Jake, what if that gets out? The killer may come back after DJ to shut him up. Oh, God." I couldn't help it. Instinctively I reached out and clutched Jake's shirt, burying my head against his solid chest. I couldn't stop shivering.

"Hey, we're not going to let anything happen to DJ. We're with him 24/7. Don't worry." His hands caressed my hair, stoking, comforting me.

For a long moment I clung to him, drawing strength from his muscular body. Then suddenly the mood changed and instead of feeling terror I felt tantalized. A creeping awareness of his solid body against mine seared through me. Heat sparked at every point our bodies touched, burning hottest in my pelvic region, sizzling moisture dampening my panties. My nipples grew stiff, my heart beat fast. Oh, God, I wanted this man.

"Say, you two, we've got this. Nobody will get to that boy."

Grant's voice shocked me like an ice water douche. I'd forgotten he was even in the room. I jumped back from Jake, stunned by the coldness that immediately shivered through me when I lost body contact with him.

"I'll just go check on him and Lily now." I made the excuse to leave the room and hustled out of the kitchen. The need to get away from Jake DeMarco was urgent.

Both children were sleeping peacefully, so I scurried on to my room. I needed to be alone, to consider those overwhelming sensations still crashing through me like cars in a demolition derby.

I tried to go to sleep. I honestly did. But I couldn't rest, couldn't stop thinking. I kept wondering if there was anything I had forgotten. The police had questioned me several times, wanting to know if I'd ever overheard any suspicious conversations, had anyone new been to the house, was Dan or Eve acting differently. I racked my brain trying to remember anything that might be helpful.

And there were those recurring thoughts of Jake. He'd been a pillar of strength throughout this ordeal. I knew he was grieving but he handled all the details and dealt with all people who called more calmly than I thought anyone could. He spent a lot of time with the kids. I know no one would believe me if I told them Jake sang off-key lullabies to his niece and blew bubbles from the balcony with his nephew. Other people didn't see that side of him. He'd probably lose his moniker of *the Playboy* if word got out he was such a softie.

Finally, I gave up trying to get to sleep and stepped out on the balcony. Maybe some fresh air would help clear my head so I could get some rest.

I had no idea Jake had the same notion. I drew in a breath when I saw him standing at the railing staring at the lake. A moonbeam shimmered over him, silver tints glinting off his cat black hair and silhouetting his muscular frame. He was clad all in black; black T-shirt skimming over muscular back and shoulders, black jeans hugging a firm ass and powerful thighs.

I tried to retreat silently to my room but he must have heard me because he suddenly swung around and called my name.

"Jenna. It's a beautiful night. Come enjoy it with me."

I followed his voice like the rats followed the Pied Piper. Some irresistible force drew me to his side. I stood next to him and raised my chin, enjoying the cooling breeze from the lake. The gentle gusts lifted my hair off my shoulders and plastered the short pink cotton gown I wore against my thighs. I couldn't think of anything to say so I stayed silent, leaning my hands against the wooden railing and staring out across the restless waters, whitecaps rippling in the moonlight.

"It's strange how the world can seem so peaceful, so normal, when our world has turned upside down, isn't it?" He kept his eyes trained on the restless waters of Lake Michigan. I heard the grief in his voice, noticed the slump of his shoulders. He put on a strong face for everyone but I felt the sadness radiating from deep within him. I reached over and covered his hand with my own, sharing the moment of mourning.

"My mom always said that when someone dies they become a star, twinkling down on us from heaven. Now there are two new stars in the sky."

Jake looked thoughtful for a moment, casting his gaze heavenwards. Then he turned and looked at me, a sad smile flitting across his chiseled features.

"I like that idea. Thank you." He touched my cheek gently with his finger. "Thank you for everything. I don't know what I would do without you."

His eyes mesmerized me and my voice caught in my throat. I wanted to tell him how that same thought had helped me deal with my own grief when my parents were murdered but I couldn't speak. The events of the last few days had brought the horror all back to me. The shock, the anger, the wondering, the endless questions. Their murders were still unsolved.

On top of the overwhelming grief and horror of their deaths, I discovered the farm was heavily mortgaged, two and three times. There was no way I could pay off the debt so I had to sell the house and land where I'd grown up, multiplying my sorrow. That's why I had to delay law school temporarily. There simply wasn't any money.

"Hey, you suddenly look like you could faint. Here. Set down." He led me over to a wicker glider and eased me down. "I'm sorry. I know this has been hard on you."

"It breaks my heart." I raised a fist to my mouth and bit on my finger. "And it brings back terrible memories. My parents were murdered two years ago."

"My God, Jenna." He sank onto the cushion next to me. "What happened?"

The story stumbled out of my mouth. It still sent pain knifing through me when I talked about it.

"And they got away with it. That's the worst part, Jake. They executed my parents and are walking around today scot free. It's not right. And I can't watch this happen again. The not knowing kills you."

Jake grabbed my shoulders and pulled me upright, his gaze locking onto my own.

"I'm not going to let it happen, Jenna. This murder is going to be solved, I vow to you." He paused and studied me for a long moment. "I promise you something else, too. When Danny and Eve's killer is caught, I'm going to have Grant investigate the death of your parents. You deserve to have answers. They deserve to have justice."

And then he kissed me.

Chapter 8: Uncontrollable Desires

Jake

I don't know why I did it. She just looked so damn desirable. Her eyes shimmered with a combination of tears and starlight, moonbeams sparking off her red gold hair. The thin pink nightgown outlined a lush figure, her body more femininely curved than the women I was usually with.

And the look on her face touched me in a different way than any other woman ever had. She looked so vulnerable, yet so courageous, so defiant. So irresistible.

I slipped my hands up to cup her cheeks and bent my head down to meet her lips. It started softly, an exploratory kiss fueled by the emotions raging in me. Once I tasted her, though, I had to have more. Passion flared and I began drinking her in. My tongue swept over her lips and she opened for me, allowing me entrance to her sweet mouth.

I don't know who groaned first, me or her, but I know we both moaned as sensations rocketed along my spine. My arms sought to draw her closer, sliding down to her waist, pulling her against me. Her skin felt hot beneath the thin fabric of her gown, silky and sensuous. I could feel the hard bud of her nipples against my chest, proof that I was not the only one turned on by the contact.

Desire flared deep in my groin, my dick stiffening to attention. God, I knew I shouldn't be doing this. This wasn't one of my fun girls, one of my playmates. I knew instinctively Jenna wasn't the type to play around or have a fling. She was the marrying kind, the type I'd always avoided.

But I wanted her. Wanted her fiercely.

She wanted me, too. I could tell. Her hands stroked through my hair and caressed my cheeks. Her body squirmed against me, a near purr emitting from her throat. Her eyes were shuttered, her long neck bent back and exposed. Her breath was coming faster, shallower.

And then the sound of a baby crying drifted through the open window.

She stiffened immediately and I saw her eyes flash open followed by a sudden look of realization. Her hands went to my chest and she pushed me firmly away, confusion painting her face.

"Lily." It was the only word she spoke before rising to her feet and scampering back indoors.

As soon as she was gone I felt more alone than I ever had before.

Weird. Definitely weird. It must be a reaction to the trauma of the past few days. I never needed anyone but for some reason when Jenna left it felt as if she dragged a piece of me with her, leaving me missing something. For a long time I just stared at the door where she had disappeared.

Jenna

I hurried toward Lily's room, becoming more grateful with every step to be removed from the danger of Jake DeMarco. What the hell had I been thinking letting him kiss me like that? Kisses meant nothing to him. He was *the Playboy* and I needed to remember that. Yes, my emotions were helter skelter these days but that was no excuse for being a dumb ass. And that's exactly what I am if I let myself get involved with a man like him.

I found Lily standing in her crib, her diaper soaking wet. Quickly I changed her and slid her into dry pajamas then sat down to rock her back to sleep. I dropped a kiss on her silky black curls, breathing in the sweet smell of her. Poor little motherless child. A fierce wave of love swept through me and I cradled her pudgy little body closer. I wish I could protect her from all the pains of the world, to keep her safe and happy. Her and DJ, too.

Thinking of DJ brought another surge of fear and I closed my eyes and whispered a brief prayer. Dear Lord, please don't let anyone find out that sweet little boy witnessed the murder. Please keep him safe from danger.

After a moment I added another thought. And please, Lord, protect me from the likes of Jake DeMarco.

The next morning Jake informed me that the coroner had released the bodies and the funeral would be held two days from now. Once again reality punched me in the gut. I just wish this nightmare would get over.

The kids and I all had a touch of cabin fever that day. DJ was sassy and wouldn't eat breakfast and the usually sunny Lily cried off and on all morning. By noon I'd had enough.

"We need a break," I announced over a lunch of grilled cheese and chicken noodle soup. "The kids and I are going to go play on the beach this afternoon. If we don't we're all going to go stir crazy."

Jake paused as he ladled another spoonful of soup into Lily's mouth.

"Are you sure that's a good idea? I've got to go the funeral home and Grant's gone following up on some interviews. There's no one to go with you."

"Jake, we'll just be at the beach right out there. We haven't left this house for five days and the kids...and I...are restless. We won't be gone long but we need some fresh air. I think it's safer than taking them out in public by myself, don't you?"

He rubbed his chin as he thought about it.

"Okay, but not for long. When I come back we can all go to town for ice cream or something."

"Deal." I smiled happily at the thought of getting out of this tension filled house even for a little while.

It was a perfect day to be on the shores of Lake Michigan. Lily, DJ, and I waded at the edge of the tumbling waters, laughing when the foam tickled our toes. We built a sand castle with three turrets and gathered pretty rocks and shells for landscaping and décor. Finally, we simply relaxed in the sun, DJ running a tiny dump truck across the sand while Lily enjoyed a bottle of water.

As usual I'd brought my binoculars with me. I loved to watch the birds soaring over the lake or get a better look at ships going past. I held the glasses to my eyes and observed a sea gull dive bombing the waves and coming up with a fish dangling from his mouth. I followed his progress as he flew towards the shore with his prize.

Wait a minute. What was that? I leaned forward, peering into the binoculars. There was a man there, half hidden behind a sand dune. Was he looking at us? I strained to see him clearer but all I could tell was he was clean shaven. A baseball cap was pulled low over his eyes and he wore a pair of dark glasses, blocking a clean view of his face. When he raised a pair of binoculars to his own eyes and looked right at me I knew. A cold shiver trickled down my spine. He was watching us.

"Time to go home, kids." I jumped to my feet and quickly gathered up our few belongings, picking Lily up in my arms and grabbing DJ's hand. My heart thundered as I hustled us across the few hundred yards to the house, glancing back over my shoulder several times to make sure no one was behind us.

"But, Jenna, I wasn't done building my road," DJ protested, dragging his feet.

"Remember, Uncle Jake's going to take us for ice cream. We have to get ready." I urged him to walk faster, fear nipping at my heels.

"Oh, yeah! Ice cream!"

Thank God the motivation worked and I managed to hurry the kids inside and lock the doors. I set the security alarm and breathed a sigh of relief. I was being silly. That man was probably just another bird watcher like me.

"Okay, bath time. Who wants to go first?"

By the time I had the sand washed off both kids and dressed in clean clothes I'd managed to calm myself down. I'd overreacted. Surely there was nothing sinister about a man on the beach with binoculars.

Chapter 9: In Deep

Jake

The afternoon at the funeral home was torturous. Danny and Eve, as young as they were, hadn't done any pre-planning as far as burial went. I had to do everything from picking out caskets to choosing clothes for them. I could handle Danny's wardrobe but I had no clue what Eve would choose to wear. Maybe I'd ask Jenna to help me with that.

By the time I finished selecting what music should be played and finalizing the obituaries I felt as if I'd been in combat. The undertaker or whoever he was danced on my nerves with his smooth talk and bereaved expression. The whole experience was surreal. Picking out caskets was especially ghoulish. It was like shopping for a new car. What upholstery for the interior, what color exterior?

As I drove back to Danny's house I felt a sense of relief wash over me. It would be good to be around the kids. They're pretty entertaining. And, I had to admit, I looked forward to being with Jenna. There is something soothing about her company, something that makes me feel calmer, better able to cope.

Yet I knew the moment I set eyes on her something was wrong. There was a tenseness in her posture, a worried look in her eyes that belied the cheerful greeting she tossed me. I shot her a curious glance but she ignored me, turning instead to straighten the tiny ponytail on Lily's head.

"I think somebody said something about ice cream earlier." Her voice was soft but I could hear stress in her tone.

"Ice cream it is. Just give me a minute to change." I studied her profile for a long moment before turning and climbing the stairs. Something was wrong. She was trying to hide it but I could tell. Funny, I'd only known her for a few days but it felt like I knew her so well.

Half hour later the four of us sat at a picnic table on the shady lot of a local ice cream parlor. DJ lapped at a huge chocolate soft serve cone and Lily dug into a bowl of strawberry. Jenna and I both sipped at chocolate malts and enjoyed the sounds of birds overhead. The kids did most of the talking, DJ, as usual asking endless questions while Lily added her own special babble to the conversation.

Soon, though, DJ grew restless and carried his cone with him as he went to explore the flower beds that surrounded the patio area. I couldn't help noticing how closely Jenna watched him, her periwinkle blue eyes never losing contact.

"Jenna." I spoke her name quietly and she turned to glance at me then immediately went back to tracking DJ's movements mixed with an occasional glance around at the other patrons.

"Jenna. What's wrong?"

"Nothing, Jake." She closed her eyes for a second. "Okay. Nothing but an overactive imagination."

"Tell me." It wasn't a request. After drawing in a long breath she told me about the man she'd seen on the beach, the uneasiness he stirred in her.

"Was he bald?"

"I couldn't tell. He had a cap on."

I took another long, slow sip of my malt and eyed her carefully. I could tell the incident had shaken her. And, I had to admit, it shook me up pretty fucking good, too. Sure, it could have been a coincidence. I just wasn't a big believer in coincidences.

Jenna

I didn't want to look into Jake's eyes. I knew what I would see there. Confirmation that I was right to be worried, that the man on the beach might not have been just a casual birdwatcher. I don't want to deal with what that could mean.

When we got home Jake grilled chicken breasts on the balcony and I tossed together a salad with a berry vinaigrette. By the time we finished eating both kids were nodding over their plates and I carted them off to tuck them in bed. When I returned to the kitchen Jake had cleared away the dirty dishes and poured a couple of glasses of wine.

"Come join me on the balcony, Jenna. We need to talk."

I didn't want to be alone with Jake DeMarco but his tone brooked no argument. I picked up a wine glass and followed him through the French doors onto the deck. The sun was just sliding under the horizon, a kaleidoscope of purples, pinks, and corals painting the skyline.

"Let's sit." Jake indicated the table and chairs and we both sat down but neither of us spoke for several minutes, just soaked in the serenity of the scene. An artist couldn't have painted a more beautiful image.

"Jenna, if this hasn't been resolved by the time the funeral is over, I think we need to take the children and go to my penthouse in Vegas."

Those were the last words I expected to come out of his mouth. We? Me? Move to Vegas? Leave Indiana? I'd never been farther away than Milwaukee.

"Are you talking about permanently?" I didn't mean to sputter but it came out that way.

"Not necessarily, but at least until they catch this guy. I don't want to take any chances with DJ's life." His coffee brown eyes took on a cold seriousness. "I think he'll be safer there. And we need you to go with us. Of course, I'll pay you extra for your trouble."

His words touched a raw nerve.

"Trouble? Taking care of DJ and Lily is not trouble. I love those kids. I can't walk away and leave them in your care. Hell, you said it yourself. How can *the Playboy* be a responsible caregiver for two toddlers?" I tried to shut my mouth but angry words kept spewing out. "I don't think dragging those babies off to Sin City is exactly what Danny and Eve had in mind when they named you guardian of their children."

Really, I can't tell you why I felt so angry at the idea of moving the kids to Nevada. I just suddenly had visions of Vegas show girls and Jake living the high life at the casinos. He'd probably have lots of drunken parties and women in his bedroom. What kind of life was that for two little kids?

"Well do you have a better suggestion?" he growled back at me. "The number one priority is to keep DJ and Lily safe. It's my opinion, and Grant's, that it would be best to get the kids away from here. Safest. It's unlikely the killer will follow us clear to Las Vegas and even if he does Grant has security guards available 24/7 there."

My shoulders slumped. I know he makes sense, but I resent his highhandedness. He could have talked to me about it first before pronouncing his decision. That's the trouble with men; they always think they know best.

"Okay. We'll go to Vegas if they haven't caught the killer by the funeral." I sounded like a sullen child but I couldn't help it. My world was turning upside down and I didn't like it. I loved those kids but I had to remember this wasn't a permanent arrangement. It was a job so I could save enough money to go to law school. And Jake had the power to dismiss me at any moment, even after I followed him and the little ones all the way to Vegas.

The problem was I grew more attached to DJ and Lily every day and, I hated to admit it, more attracted to their uncle.

One thought kept repeating in my mind.

The only possible ending to this situation was heartbreak for me.

Chapter 10: A Changed Man

Jake

Jenna was pissed but damn it, I had to do what I thought was necessary to keep my nephew safe. Until the bastard that killed my brother and his wife was put away DJ's life could be in danger. Hell, I didn't want to leave either. I wanted to stay right here and find the mother fucker responsible for tearing up my world, for taking away those kids' parents, for killing my only brother and his wife.

Suddenly she spoke in a quiet voice.

"If we have to go to Vegas, I have one request."

"What?"

"Well, uh." She hesitated, the rosy red color flooding her cheeks obvious even in the twilight. You could almost see her building up her courage.

"I want you to promise you won't bring your...lifestyle ...around the kids. Your parties and your, uh, women."

She looked so pious there for a moment I would have laughed if I hadn't been so offended. What kind of guy did she think I was? Then I sobered for a moment. I did have a reputation and obviously it had preceded me. She was only trying to protect the kids in her own way.

"Jenna. Look at me." I waited until she turned her head and faced me, her chin rising in that way I now recognized as a sign of determination.

"Trust me. I wouldn't do that. Besides, I won't be doing any partying until this is resolved. I can't rest until that bastard is arrested."

And there was something Jenna didn't know. Something so horrific I hated to contemplate it. The thought brought me to my feet and I strode to the railing, nearly overcome by emotion. I tilted my head back and gazed at the darkening sky, the moon creeping higher over the lake. I drew in a couple of long shuddering breaths as I tried to calm myself. I didn't want to lose it now, not with Jenna watching.

I didn't realize she had come up beside me until she spoke softly and touched my hand.

"Jake." My name was just a whisper but I could hear the feelings in it. The concern, the shared pain. The simple gesture of laying her hand on mine spoke volumes. "There's more than you've told me, isn't there?"

I was famous for my poker face but apparently it wasn't working tonight. I didn't want to look at her, didn't want her to see my pain, the secret gnawing at my gut. Yet something compelled me to tell her. I guess I just needed to share it with someone.

"The autopsy report showed Eve was eight weeks pregnant."

I heard her sharp intake of breath, felt her fingers grip my hand tightly. Her shoulders slumped and she dropped her head.

"Oh, God. The baby." The words choked in her throat and shudders racked her body. Her knees started to buckle and I wrapped my arms around her to support her.

Her hands gripped my T-shirt in clenched fists and her head fell against my chest. I felt her tears soaking into my shirt as she cried soundlessly, her shoulders shaking. All I could do was hold her, my hand stroking the length of her silky tresses, murmuring incoherent words of comfort.

"God, this nightmare just keeps getting worse, Jake. That baby's life ended before it even started."

"I know, honey, I know." The endearment slipped out, sounding as if I were comforting someone DJ's age but there was nothing childlike about her body pressed tightly against mine. Lord, she felt good. Strong and real. There was nothing artificial about this woman. Even her hair was its natural color. She didn't fake emotions. She wasn't like the parade of Barbie dolls I'd spent time with the last few years. With them everything was phony from their eyelashes to their Botox-filled lips. Jenna was all real.

Especially those melon-sized boobs pressing into my shirtfront.

Jenna tilted her face up towards mine, teardrops on the tips of her long, spikey lashes.

"God, Jake, so much death. So damn much death." She closed her eyes tight against the pain and new rivulets squeezed out beneath her lids. Lord, she'd been through hell and back. First her own parents, now this. Did I even have the right to ask her to keep putting herself through this? To remain shrouded in murder mysteries? Should I release her from her promise to stay with the kids?

But I knew even if she removed herself far, far away from the situation, she wouldn't forget. She'd still be haunted by the nightmares, still tormented by not knowing who or why. She'd worry constantly about the kids, too. She wasn't a flighty party girl who would just scamper away and dissolve her worries in a bottle or a bed.

No, she was better off here, with the kids, with me. With the one person who understood exactly what she was feeling.

Wasn't she?

Jenna

The news of Eve's pregnancy shook me to my core, emotions flaring like wild fires spontaneously combusting. Anger, grief, confusion, all those feelings and more battled within me. I clung to Jake for strength because I suddenly felt so weak, so helpless. I couldn't make things right; I couldn't undo the evil that had been done. I couldn't even punish the people responsible for the holocaust.

I cried, unable to stop the flood of feelings crashing within me. I cried for Danny and Eve, I cried for DJ and Lily and the baby who never got a chance to live. I wept for my Mom and Dad. And I cried for me. I felt lost, like I was adrift in the middle of Lake Michigan.

Slowly, though, I became aware of another feeling; the sensation of Jake's body pressed to mine. I had his shirt clutched in my fists, my head buried against the rock hard muscles of his chest. I could hear his heart thumping beneath my ear.

That heartbeat. The sound of life. I needed to hear that, to drown out the silence of death. I needed to feel alive.

I tilted my head back and blinked my tears away so I could look into his eyes. I saw my own jumble of emotions reflected in their depths.

I tried to fight the sudden urge that filled me but I couldn't stop myself. My hands reached up and clasp his neck and I pull his head down, my lips seeking his. I need to taste him, to breathe his breath, to drink in his aliveness.

His arms tighten around my waist and pull me closer to the length of him. He kisses me back with a hungry passion that urges me on. My hands slide farther up, digging into his thick mop of cat black curls, raking through the silky mop.

He pulled back and I groan, but he was gone only long enough to move his mouth to my neck, his lips like velvet against my skin, skimming a trail along my throat. The tip of his tongue glazed the hollow of my neck and I shiver, moisture soaking my panties.

"God, Jake, make me feel alive." My words sounded almost like a prayer. I need to feel life humming through my veins, need to stamp out the shadow of death darkening my world. Alright, I admit it; I need Jake DeMarco, his strength, his vitality. God help me, I need *the Playboy*.

And that's when he swept me off my feet and lifted all 159 pounds of me into his arms.

Chapter 11: Innocence Meets Experience

Jake

Hell's bells. Did she know what she was doing to me? When she told me to make her feel alive all common sense flew out of my head. I didn't stop to think, to remind myself that this was a very bad idea. That this was the nanny. I just picked her up in my arms and started towards my room.

Thank God the kids were asleep and Grant was gone to the casino to talk to some of Danny's cohorts. I wanted nothing more than to be alone with this woman.

"Jake, put me down. I'm too heavy." She wrapped her arms tight around my neck and squirmed but it just turned me on more.

"You're not too heavy. You're perfect." I used my foot to kick open the bedroom door, carried her to the bed, and gently laid her down. Her eyes immediately went to the skylight overhead, her gaze widening at the view of stars floating against a backdrop of midnight blue.

I never even looked up. All my eyes wanted to see was Jenna there on that big soft mattress. God, she's beautiful. Spicy and bold, her rusty red curls splayed on the white pillow case, her long sun kissed legs exposed beneath the hem of the short coral colored dress she wore. She looked like a painting, a portrait of the essence of womanhood. Lush feminine curves wrapped in the scintillating scent of sunshine and citrus blossoms.

And then I realized she also looked vulnerable and innocent. Tear stains still trailed down her cheeks, clear periwinkle blue eyes reflecting the shine of the stars through the skylight. The only makeup she wore was a rosy pink gloss that made her mouth look moist and desirable...yet it still trembled from her bout of weeping.

Damn, I'm a fucking bastard. I have no right to take advantage of this girl just because she's upset and grieving. What am I thinking? Well, apparently, I'm not...at least not with my big head. This was Jenna, not an airheaded poker groupie or a gold digger who slept with a different man every night. She wasn't like the usual stream of females that flowed in and out of my life. And, I have to live with her for who knows how long. Things might get pretty awkward if I followed through with the desire that had been building in me ever since I laid eyes on this unique woman.

Fuck. Since when had I become a gentleman? But I couldn't do this with a clear conscience. Immediately after the thought my dick protested, throbbing hungrily. Shut up, Johnson, I silently ordered it. Unfortunately, it wasn't very good at taking orders.

But I know I'm not the right kind of man for Jenna. I'm not the staying kind. She deserves better than me.

I dropped to my knees next to the bed and picked her hand up in mine, my gaze trapped in those violet blue eyes. I had to take a long, deep breath in order to force the words out of my mouth.

"Jenna, I can't believe I'm saying this, but I don't want to take advantage of you. You're upset, you're sad, and you're emotional. I would like nothing more than to make love to you but I'm afraid. Afraid I'm being selfish, afraid tomorrow you'll wake up and regret our time together. Regret that I'm not a man who knows how to have a real relationship."

Jenna

I raised my hand and cupped his cheek. If I'm honest, I have to admit I'm afraid of that, too, but I'd never felt such a strong need before. I know Jake may never be a one-woman man but I still want him. At least this one time. Hell, I wasn't ready to jump into any long-term commitments, either.

"Jake, you are a sweet, honest man and I respect that. But I know what I'm doing. I have plans of my own. I'm going to law school. I'm going to be a prosecuting attorney so I can stop scum like the people who killed my parents, who murdered Danny and Eve. I'm not asking for a lifetime. I'm just asking for tonight."

I hope I didn't sound like I was begging. I wasn't. I just wanted to let him know I wasn't going into this blind, that I didn't expect anything in the future. I'm not a romantic and I wasn't staking a claim. But I still needed him, wanted him, still needed to feel life surging through me. Sex with Jake would surely be the world's best stress reliever. I could lose myself in him and forget this nightmare at least for a little while.

He stared into my eyes for a long solemn moment before groaning and gathering me to him, his lips seeking mine.

"Lord, forgive me, I can't resist you." He whispered the words in between kisses, devouring me, nipping, tasting. I wrapped one arm around his neck and splayed the other hand on his chest, glorying in the feel of the hot, hard surface beneath the cool cotton of his shirt. I let my own lips wander along his jawline, feeling the scrape of his day old beard against my cheek, running my hand across his neck. His curls played against my fingers, begging me to caress the back of his head.

His hand burned into the skin at my waist. The cotton knit dress I wore did little to cool the flames he ignited everywhere he touched. Heat radiated through me as his lips skimmed downward, his tongue tickling the cleavage exposed by the scooped neckline of my dress.

I can't stop my hands from exploring his body. I run my palms across his shoulders and up and down his back. He's all corded muscle without an excess pound of flesh on his body. Like velvet covered steel.

And then I want to see that body, not just feel it. I eagerly pulled his shirt out of his jeans and plunged my hands upwards, shoving and tugging at the fabric until he raised his arms and pulled it over his head.

"Damn." I drew in a deep breath at the sight of him. "You're beautiful."

He chuckled and kissed my forehead.

"That's my line, honey. You're beautiful."

I smiled and buried my head in his chest before giving his nipple a playful nip. But one taste wasn't enough and I found myself circling the pebbled bud with my tongue, swirling and flicking at its hard tip. He shuddered and his hand swept up to cup my breast, his thumb stroking my own engorged nipple.

Gradually he eased me back until my head rested on the pillows. He stroked my hair from my face, his gaze meeting mine with hot tenderness. He bent forward and captured my lips again, his tongue tracing their outline with maddening gentleness. His hand found its way back to my breast but this time he slipped his fingers under the neckline of my dress and beneath the silky fabric of my bra.

It was like an electric shock when he grasped my nipple between his thumb and forefinger and tweaked it. My hips reared off the bed and a moan scraped from my throat. Oh, God, I could feel the contraction in my uterus as liquid gushed between my legs.

Then his fingers plucked at the ribbons that held the front of my dress closed, loosening them until he could shove the fabric apart and down my shoulders. He urged my hips up as he pulled the dress lower and slid it off my feet.

As I lay there in just my peach silk bra and panties I was shocked by how natural it felt. Usually I was shy about my body, knowing it wasn't as thin as most men liked. Yet the look on Jake's face reassured me that he wasn't disappointed. I see the admiration and desire burning in his eyes and it builds a new confidence in me. I can't help but tease him a bit and give a sensuous writhe while lifting my hair and letting it slide through my fingers.

God, I want this man like I've never wanted a man before.

Chapter 12: All The Way

Jake

She's a temptress, a siren calling me to her with an irresistible song. I drank in the sight of her displayed there under the skylight, all that smooth golden skin, those hour glass curves. Her breasts swelled above the cups of her bra, begging to be released. Slowly, almost reverently I reached out and undid the front clasp of the garment, revealing the magnificent mounds.

Wow. Full and round with protruding rock hard nipples and rosy pink aureoles. Definitely silicone free. I don't think I've ever seen a more beautiful pair. My mouth watered just thinking about feasting on them. Then I stopped thinking about it and took action, leaning down to swath my tongue across that swollen bud before drawing it into the depths of my mouth.

So sweet. I cupped my hand and filled it with the warm flesh, wondering at the silky smoothness of it. My other hand glided downward, savoring the feel of her skin. She shivered and squirmed as my palm glided over her abdomen. My dick grew even harder, pressing against her silky panties. I pushed my knee between her legs and she opened for me. My fingers skimmed the edge of her panties until I worked them lower and lower, slowly revealing the view of her femininity. She was all natural here, too, with a tapering crop of soft auburn curls. Beautiful.

"Please."

Her voice was a whimper of need and I responded, pushing her panties farther down her legs and sliding my hand into her hidden valley. God, she was soaking wet. When my finger slid across the top of her clit she moaned and heaved her hips upwards, her pelvis twisting. I did it again, slower, teasing, tempting.

I watched her face as the sensations built within her. Her eyes closed and her hands bit into my ribs. Lord, she was already going to come. I massaged her clit with swirling circles of my thumb and let my middle digit slide to her damp entrance and slip inside.

As I did she cried out and her vaginal muscles cramped around my finger, contracting and releasing with intensity. She threw her head back against the pillows, exposing her long neck and I bent to kiss her there. Her arms latched onto my shoulders, clinging as she spasmed. Moisture flooded my hand and the sweet scent of her musk tinged the air.

"Jake. God, Jake."

"Let go, baby. Let it all go, Jenna." I urged her on taking a unique pleasure in watching her detonate before me.

Her body arched and a keening sound came from her throat as I shoved a second finger inside her, my thumb never stopping its motion against her clit. Her nails raked into my back, streaking downward to clutch my ass.

"God, Jake, I need you now. I need you in me. And you're still dressed."

I made quick work of shedding my jeans and briefs, taking a moment to retrieve a condom out of the dresser drawer. I cuddled her sumptuous body against me, reveling in the feeling of her warm, soft flesh. Hot damn, what a woman.

Now her hands were roaming all over me, stroking my back, my butt, zeroing in on my rock hard dick. She gasped when she felt the length and girth of it, a startled look shooting across her face.

"My God, you're humongous. I've never..." her voice faded away but I could hear the tension in it.

"Shh, Jenna. It'll be all right. I won't hurt you."

Her fingers stroked the length of my cock and it pulsated in her hand. Her thumb grazed across the tip and creamy liquid bubbled up. She spread it across the head of my dick then slid her hand all the way down to my balls.

Now it was my turn to groan. She was driving me mad. Quickly I grabbed the condom and ripped the foil packet open. When she took it out of my hand and rolled it down the length of my dick I almost came right then.

My lips hungered for hers. I kissed her with a passion that came from my soul. Gliding my hand down the naked skin of her spine to find her voluptuous ass. I squeezed and molded the firm mound, pressing my cock against her pubis.

I couldn't wait any more. I pushed her legs farther open and paused at the entrance to her womanhood. I felt her tense momentarily but I held back. I didn't want to hurt her, but the need to be inside her battered me. Slowly I pushed the head of my dick into her pussy just an inch or two, her gasp audible as her flesh spread to welcome me.

I forced myself to hold still for a moment before I lifted her legs and she wrapped them around my waist. Then I drove smoothly, gradually, into her depths until I felt the head of my prick knock against her cervix.

God, she was so tight. So damn, deliciously tight.

I eased my prick backwards then thrust forward again.

Lord, I'm usually known for my stamina but two strokes and I was ready close come.

Jenna

At first I thought his hard cock wasn't going to fit but gradually my body opened to accommodate his bulk. He filled me completely, my flesh quivering, clenching his dick within me. Sweet Jesus he was big.

That was my last coherent thought before my mind shut down and my body took control. My heels dug into his ass, my fingers tunneled into his back. My hips rose to meet his every stroke and I couldn't conceive of anything outside of this bed this moment with this man.

Every one of my senses was alive. I bit into his shoulder, tasting his sweet hot flesh. The spicy scent of him filled my nose with manly fragrance and I felt the sturdy length of him impaling me.

My gaze locked onto his eyes, watching the play of emotions across his face. His lids lowered to half-mast, a glaze of pure pleasure shadowing their depths.

"God, Jenna, you feel so good."

His words came out as a groan. I could only moan in response.

With a quick, smooth motion he rolled us over and I found myself on top. I bent forward, my boobs grazing across his chest and grabbed his hands for support. My hair draped around his face. I felt powerful, in control. It was my turn to set the pace, to raise and lower my hips in a tantalizing tempo.

Soon, though, I lost that control. Passion was the driving force, blinding me, deafening me as a whirlwind of sensations swirled through my body. I'd never experienced such a powerful force before this man.

Now there were no longer two of us; just one being magically blended into harmonious vibrations. Our orgasms grew together, building, swelling until there was one massive explosion as we came simultaneously. I cried out and so did he as I rode him like a bucking bronco, boobs bouncing, heart racing. His hands clenched my butt cheeks and held me still and I felt his dick throbbing as he came.

Spasms racked my body, colors exploded before my eyes. The sensations went on and on and I wished they would never stop. I arched my back, and closed my eyes, giving myself completely to the moment.

Damn. I said I wanted to feel alive.

I sure in the hell got my wish.

Chapter 13: The Morning After

Jake

Holy crap! What the hell just happened? Jenna had rocked my world. As she lay cuddled close beside me, her breath coming in labored gasps I knew something was different. I'd had sex with dozens of women, including show girls, celebrities, top models, even a princess.

But something was different this time. A feeling that went deeper than sexual satisfaction...something foreign, unfamiliar.

Something downright scary.

My hand stroked her silky hair where it spread across my chest and a strange tenderness welled inside me. This was Jenna, the woman who shared so many things with me; my grief, my love for my niece and nephew, a home, and now a bed I wasn't in any hurry for her to get out of.

And that was probably the biggest difference of all. Usually I didn't want to linger. I rarely spent the entire night with a woman, permanently prepared with a good excuse to leave or to send her on her way. I always remembered them the next day with flowers and a gift. And then I seldom saw them again.

That wasn't going to happen this time. I would see Jenna in the morning and for an unknown number of tomorrows in the future. The weird part was, I kind of liked the idea.

When I woke up, she was gone. The place where she had lain felt cold and empty. Why the hell did that bother me so much?

I climbed out of bed and headed for the shower, my hard dick standing up straight, memories of last night's activities fueling its hunger. God, better make that a cold shower.

When I finished and dressed I found Jenna in the kitchen. She was at the counter stirring up waffle batter, her booty wiggling as she worked the whisk. Lily was in her high chair and DJ played on the floor nearby, rolling a miniature John Deere tractor across the wood.

I wasn't particularly pleased to see Grant setting at the table, his gaze feasting on Jenna's denim clad bottom, a smile playing across his lips. I could practically read his dirty mind.

"Morning, everybody. Morning, Lilybell." I bent and kissed the top of my niece's head, reached down to tousle DJs hair, and headed for the coffee pot. "Something smells mighty good in here, Jenna."

She didn't turn to look at me and I saw pink stain paint her cheeks.

"Bacon's in the oven. Have a seat. This is just about done."

"Yeah, come join me, Jake." Grant invited. "By the way, I'd like to talk to you after breakfast. In the office."

Grant's tone told me he had something serious to discuss. I wanted to tell him to forget food, just spill his guts and let me know what he found out but the kids didn't need to hear it. It could wait a few more minutes.

As usual the meal Jenna prepared was delicious but I really couldn't do it justice. I was too curious about what Grant had to tell me. That, and the fact that Jenna still hadn't really looked at me played havoc with my appetite.

Grant didn't seem to have any problems in that department. He scarfed everything Jenna set before him, all the while complimenting her cooking, even giving her a wink. Grant may be one of my best friends but at that moment I wanted to punch him in his handsome face.

"You done yet, Grant? If you are, let's move to the office."

I didn't look to see if he was following me, just took off down the hall. I didn't sit at Danny's desk but chose to stand in front of the window instead, fastening my gaze on the serenity of the lake, sun glinting on the rolling waves.

I heard Grant close the door and turned to face him.

"Okay, what have you got?"

He'd gathered quite a bit of information. I may not appreciate his interest in Jenna but I had to say he earned his money as an investigator. Turned out Danny's old friend Reno Vasquez had a rock solid alibi. He told Grant he found religion in prison and now was a street corner preacher, but that night he'd been in the hospital undergoing emergency surgery to remove his appendix.

"Damn." I rapped my knuckles on the desk top. "I was sure Reno was involved in this somehow. What else?"

Grant heard Danny was playing regularly at the local casino so he'd spent last night talking to people there. He said more than one guy told him Danny had been losing frequently to one of the high rollers. Thought he might owe him money.

"The guy has a full head of hair, though." The investigator ran his hand through his own sandy locks. "Course, he could have paid a bald guy to do the dirty work."

He'd checked on the bald employees at the restaurant and each of them had been ruled out. The manager, Joe Fielder, admitted to spending the night with Eve's sister Tarina and she confirmed it. Interesting.

But there was nothing that pointed directly at the answer to the big question. Who killed Danny and Eve?

Jenna

I couldn't face Jake that morning, couldn't let him see how much last night had moved me. I didn't know it could be like that, so intense, a sharing so intimate it reached your very core. I promised him I wouldn't get attached, but damn, I knew now once would never be enough with Jake DeMarco.

But it was going to have to be.

Breakfast was a tense affair with Grant talking way too much and Jake barely speaking. I heaved a sigh of relief when the meal was over and the men left the room.

It was going to be a busy day. The funeral was tomorrow. The maid service was coming this afternoon to clean the house and prepare it for the reception that would be held here after the burial. Danny's restaurant was catering the meal and providing the wait staff.

Jake had asked me to choose something for Eve to wear and I laid out the rose silk dress I had selected so he could take it to the funeral home. Eve looked beautiful in that color. I added a diamond heart necklace and a pair of diamond studs. Simple yet elegant. I had to turn away before my tears stained the fabric.

Jake and I had decided it would be best if the children didn't attend the funeral, so I would stay home with them. We still had to have clothes ready for the reception so I made sure everything was clean and pressed. I was just coming out of the laundry room when I ran smack into Jake.

Crashing into Jake DeMarco was like hitting a wall. A solid wall of rock hard muscle. The force of the collision sent me swaying back on my heels and Jake grabbed my arms before I fell. Fire blazed to life in my blood, heat burning my cheeks.

"Fancy running into you here." He grinned, his hands still gripping my wrists. "Tell me, Jenna, have you been avoiding me this morning?"

I did my best to appear nonchalant.

"Not all. I've been busy, you've been busy."

I gave a slight tug to my arms and he let them go. My flesh still burned where his touch had been.

"Please don't be uncomfortable. Last night was beautiful."

"Just don't let it happen again, right?" I tilted my head, my chin raised. "I told you I didn't expect anything from you and I don't. Now if you don't mind I need to get lunch started. Soup and sandwiches okay with you?"

After lunch Jake left to deliver the clothing to the funeral home and I put the kids down for their nap. I was alone with my thoughts for a while. I tried to concentrate on anything other than Jake DeMarco but I wasn't very successful. Images of his naked body kept floating through my mind, wreaking havoc with my senses.

That evening Jake went to the casino with Grant, deciding to set in on a few games with the high rollers Danny had been playing with and see if he could learn anything more. I was grateful when they left and I was alone with the sleeping children. I soaked in a hot tub for a long time, thinking about the changes that would come if we were forced to go to Las Vegas. The children would be leaving everything they knew behind; their home, their neighborhood and friends, their Aunt Tarina. Jake and I would be the only familiar figures in their lives.

My life would change completely, too. I'd never lived in a big city before, let alone in a penthouse atop a world famous casino. How would a country girl like me fit in in Sin City? And more importantly, how would I live with Jake DeMarco every day and not give in to the irresistible craving to have sex with him again?

He was like crack cocaine or heroin. One time and I was hooked, hungering for another fix. He was addictive and he was dangerous. Lord, give me strength to conquer this desire.

Chapter 14: Old Debts

Jake

"So, how much did my brother owe you?"

I had no problem joining the game with Wade Holland, the high roller Grant said Danny was in debt to. My reputation preceded me and I was welcomed warmly by the staff and patrons on the gambling boat.

Now I sat at the poker table with Holland and one other player, Norm, a nerdy looking guy with coke bottle glasses and acne scars. I had a big stack of chips in front of me and the nerd had just shoved his puny stack all in. I had a pair of queens in my hand and another lady had been dealt on the flop. I was confident as I called his bet.

My three of a kind easily beat his pair of aces and then it was just me and Holland left at the table.

"Ah, he was only into me about a hundred grand." Holland studied his newly dealt cards and played with his chips. "I wasn't worried about it. Danny always paid up in the long run."

As a poker player I'd gotten pretty good at reading faces and the slight tension around Holland's mouth and eyes told me he was probably lying. I glanced at the two hold cards I'd been dealt. A queen and king of spades. I shoved chips to the center of the table and raised the bet.

Holland moved slowly, fiddling with his chips before calling. The dealer made the flop. A jack and ten of spades and an ace of hearts. I called and Holland raised. I met his raise and waited patiently for the dealer to flip over the next card. It was a ten of clubs.

"I was sorry to hear about what happened to Danny and his lady." Holland ran his hand through his thick crop of silver curls. "A damn shame."

He said the right words but they didn't sound sincere to me. I just nodded and waited for the dealer to play the last card. The ace of spades. I had a royal flush. Hot damn.

There was silence at the table for a long moment, and then Holland shoved his stack of chips to the middle of the table.

"I'm all in."

"Call."

A gleeful smile split Holland's fat face, a greedy gleam lighting up his small blue eyes.

"Full house."

I sat there silent as a stone, letting my shoulders fall in a defeated slump.

"Damn. All I've got is a royal flush."

A quick flash of rage shot from his eyes before he disguised it. He rose from the table and offered me his hand.

"Good game, DeMarco."

"Thanks." I counted out a hundred thousand dollars' worth of chips from my winnings and shoved them towards him with a steely glance. "Consider Danny's debt paid in full."

"You don't have to do that. It wasn't your debt."

"It was a DeMarco debt."

I left the table without another word and went to find Grant. I'd had enough. I was ready to go back to the house. I just wished Jenna would meet me in my room when I got there.

Don't be a fool. I scolded myself harshly for even thinking about the prospect. That wasn't going to happen, not tonight, not ever again. I needed to stay away from that woman. She's poison to a man like me. She was a keeper, as they say. But he didn't want any woman on a permanent basis. He was the Playboy; he had a reputation to maintain. Nothing would put a cramp in his lifestyle the way a woman like Jenna would.

No. He needed to remember. She was the nanny. Just the nanny.

Jenna

I didn't sleep well that night. I lay awake listening for Jake to come home, tension filling my muscles. Tomorrow was going to be a hard day, the day Danny and Eve were laid to rest. There would be dozens of people arriving at the house after they left the cemetery. How would DJ and Lily respond to the crowd? Would they sense the somberness of the occasion?

My heart went out to Jake as well. I knew the funeral would be a distressing experience for him. It wasn't that long ago that I'd been on the receiving end of all those pitying looks, heard all the condolences, all the while knowing every one of those people were thanking God it wasn't them in that position. It hadn't been their loved ones murdered.

When I heard Jake come in it was nearly two o'clock. I held my breath, afraid that he would come to my door, afraid that he wouldn't. When several minutes passed I relaxed. I wouldn't have to face my demons tonight.

The morning brought overcast skies and the distant rumble of thunder. Appropriate funeral weather. It matched my mood.

I stood in the shower for a long time just letting the water stream over my tired body, hoping it would wash away the shroud of exhaustion cloaking me. I slept little last night, my slumber disturbed by vivid dreams.

Visions of garish neon lights flashed over the dead bodies of Danny and Eve as they spun on a roulette table and the sound of crying children surrounded me. When that scene disappeared it morphed into images of a naked Jake at a poker table playing cards with a bevy of beautiful show girls. Two exotic looking women stood behind him rubbing his shoulders, running their hands through his hair and across his chest. Everyone was drinking champagne, laughing and flirting. And Jake, the rat bastard, was enjoying every second of the lavish attention.

I know it's stupid, but I still felt pissed off. Seeing him with those other women, even if it was only in a dream, disturbed me more than I liked to admit. Wow, I really needed an attitude adjustment…fast.

Jake had to be at the funeral home by ten that morning so I hurried to get breakfast ready. Quickly I mixed up a batch of banana nut muffins and stuck them in the oven then started the coffee. It was just beginning to stream into the pot when I heard Lily cry and scurried in to get her up and changed. DJ stumbled into her room a moment later, holding his rabbit by the ear and rubbing his eyes with one small fist.

"Okay, guys, let's get some breakfast." I herded the kids down the hall but stopped short when I saw Jake walking into the kitchen from the other direction.

The breath I drew in was so sharp it was almost painful. *Daaammm*. Jake always looked good but dressed in his tailor made black suit, white shirt, and silver silk tie he looked like he'd just walked off the cover of GQ magazine. The perfect image of a suave, sophisticated man about town. A man so far out of my league he might as well live on another planet.

I busied myself getting the kids into their seats and passing out sippy cups filled with milk. The timer went off on the oven and I pulled the fragrant muffins out and sat them on the counter to cool. Now I would just whip up some scrambled eggs and...

"Morning, Jenna." The sound of Jake's deep voice made me jump. I didn't realize he had walked up behind me. "I need a coffee cup."

He reached around me to the cupboard overhead, his scent even more delicious than that of the fresh baked muffins. His hip brushed against me as he retrieved his mug and a quiver shot along my spine. Ah, hell. I had to get over those kinds of reactions every time he came near.

I forced my attention back to whipping the eggs and pouring them in the frying pan, praying he'd move away and give me more space. It was hard to breathe when he was this close. Fortunately, Grant chose that moment to enter the room and Jake turned to speak to him so I managed to get breakfast on the table without hyperventilating.

I got the kids fed then settled them in the adjoining family room with a set of blocks to play with. Grant and Jake were still seated at the kitchen table when Jake called me over.

"Sit down, Jenna. We need to talk about this afternoon."

"I just want to ask you to keep your eyes and ears wide open during the reception." Grant took another sip of coffee then continued. "We're pretty sure Danny knew his killer so it's possible it's someone who will come to the funeral. Somebody who might be missed if they didn't show up. Or somebody who just wants to see the results of his handiwork."

I'd seen enough crime dramas on TV and read enough murder mysteries to know he was right. The possibility that the killer might be right here in this house later this afternoon hit me like a punch in the gut.

"DJ" was the only word I spoke.

Chapter 15: Getting On With It

Jake

I watched the color drain out of Jenna's face and heard the fear in her voice when she whispered my nephew's name. I reached out and covered her hand with mine to still the trembling of her fingers.

"Don't worry. Detective Wayne and some of his men will be here and we'll all keep an eye on DJ. Chances are nothing will happen. We just want you to be alert and pay attention to what goes on around you."

She squared her shoulders and gave me a small smile and a nod, her chin tilting up in that determined look I'd come to recognize.

"Okay. Well, we better get going then." Grant rose to his feet. "I think I'll grab an umbrella, though. Looks like we're going to need it."

Grant strode out of the room and I stood as well. Jenna rose at the same time and laid her hand on my arm. I saw the emotions in her eyes as her irises deepened to almost grape colored. She didn't have to say a word. Her eyes said it all for her, signaled her sympathy but more than that, her understanding of just how painful this moment is. Losing a loved one to any type of death is hard, but losing them at the hands of a murderer only made it tougher, especially when you had no answers to the ceaseless barrage of questions rocketing though your mind.

With a quick hard motion, I pulled her to me and let myself drown in those purple pools. I followed my urge to lower my head and take possession of her lips, drawing strength from their velvety heat.

"Don't worry, Jen. We'll get through this."

Then I turned and walked out the door.

Jenna

The house felt empty after the men left for the funeral home. Even the kids were quiet as they played in the family room. I knew it would be at least five hours before guests began to arrive but the catering crew would be here earlier. In the meantime, I planned on quiet time with the kids then a bit of lunch and a quick nap before I dressed them for company.

I just finished putting the kids down when the first van pulled into the drive. Elegant gold letters declared DeMarco's against glossy black paint. I watched out the window as the driver, a short, stocky bald man climbed out and headed for the door.

The man was Joe Fielder, the manager of the restaurant. We spoke for a minute. He was personable and seemed competent, taking charge the minute the next van pulled up. In no time the crew had taken over the kitchen and began to set out buffet tables.

While they were busy doing that I made my escape so I could get dressed. I slipped on a simple little black dress and kitten heeled black sandals, pulling my hair up in a loose knot and adding a pair of onyx studs. A couple strokes of mascara and some lip gloss and I was as ready as I was going to get.

The place was a beehive of activity when I returned to the kitchen. Servers clad in gold shirts and black pants or skirts hustled around laying out stacks of plates and silverware. A huge pot of coffee sat on one table next to a big vat of ice tea while in the family room a bar had been set up and stocked. Trays filled with appetizers and chafing dishes offering a variety of hot treats covered the dining room table. Joe Fielder seemed to be everywhere, clipping out orders and tweaking minute details.

"This is for Danny and Eve, everybody. Let's do it right." Joe's shouted words to his crew touched my heart and I felt tears sting my eyes. Quickly I hurried away to check on the kids before I started crying like a baby myself.

I'd just finished getting Lily and DJ dressed when Detective Wayne and a couple other plain clothes officers arrived. A few minutes later Jake and Grant turned up accompanied by Eve's sister Tarina. I'd met the skinny young woman a few times before but I wasn't quite sure what to think of her. She seemed a bit of a wild child to me, complete with tattoos and piercings. Eve had confided in me that Tarina had battled with drugs, heroin in particular, but was now supposedly clean and sober.

She didn't look very straight to me but maybe her eyes were so red from crying and her nervous movements caused by tension. She just seemed so different from the fresh faced Eve with her happy smile and classic beauty. It was hard to believe they were sisters. Tarina looked like a hooker as far as I was concerned, even today. Her black dress was a clinging jersey knit and ended well above her knees, made even shorter by the sky high stilettos she wore. Her mop of too black hair was long and nearly stick straight. Her skin was deeply bronzed. I suppose some people find her heavily lined and shadowed dark brown eyes exotic but to me it was all just a bit much.

She reminded me of Elvira, that witchy woman who hosted horror movies on TV.

The kids loved her though. Lily eagerly went into her arms and DJ shouted with delight when he saw her.

"Hey, Aunt Rina! Want to play hide and seek again?" DJ jumped up and down with enthusiasm.

"Sure, buddy, but not right now, okay? I've got to do some boring old grown up stuff first. Then we'll play. How's that?"

DJ frowned in disappointment but grumbled his assent. "But don't forget! You promised."

Tarina held up her hand for a high five and DJ hopped up to slap her palm.

"All right, big guy. I'll see you in a bit. Right now, I could use a drink. Here you go, Lily. Go back to Jenna." Lily happily retreated to my arms and Tarina made a beeline for the bar.

Lily squirmed to get down so I let her stand on her own two little feet.

"Bites," she announced and toddled determinedly towards the kitchen.

"Hold on there, missy," I called before turning to urge DJ to follow. Obviously Lily was on a mission to find some food.

The next couple hours I herded DJ and Lily around the crowded house. It seemed like every guest wanted a moment with the kids. Some of them were too loud and jolly while others cooed over them with tears in their eyes, surrounded by a sorrowful aura. The kids responded well, even to the overly dramatic, charming everyone with their adorable faces and apple-cheeked smiles, but after a while I could tell they were beginning to get worn out by the crowd. I recognized Lily's rubbing of her eyes as the telltale sign she was sleepy and made our excuses to leave.

To my surprise Tarina appeared at my side as I was carrying Lily to her room with DJ at my side.

"I hope you don't mind if I tag along." The look on her face said she really didn't care if I minded or not. "I'd like to spend a little more time with my niece and nephew. Maybe I can help put Lily down."

"Of course." How could I say no to their aunt, even if I didn't think she was the best role model in the world? She was Eve's sister and the children's only maternal aunt. She had a right to spend as much time with them as she wished.

I led the way into Lily's room and changed her diaper before tucking her in with a bottle of water and her favorite blankie. I rubbed her belly for a moment and watched her eyes flutter shut. Such an angel baby.

When I turned around to face Tarina and DJ, I found them whispering together, their heads bent close to each other.

"Jenna, me and Aunt Rina want to play hide and go seek." DJ didn't ask, just stated the information in a matter of fact tone.

My first instinct was to veto the idea. I needed to keep DJ in sight. I couldn't let him wander off on his own. Not when a murderer might be in the house; make that a murderer whose next target might be DJ.

"We play every time I come." Tarina's tone was almost defiant, daring me to try and supersede her rights. I wasn't sure what to do. Then it came to me.

"Okay, DJ. That's fine. But I want to play, too. I'll be on your team, okay?"

"Okay." DJ grinned and offered me a fist bump.

"Cool."

"Okay. I'm going to hide first." Tarina jumped to her feet and clapped her hands in a childlike gesture. "Don't forget to sing Twinkle, Twinkle Little Star three times before you start looking for me."

And then she was gone.

Chapter 16: Saying Goodbye

Jake

This had been the hardest day of my life. I had a moment alone with Danny and Eve before the official visitation started. As I stood there by their caskets, their familiar but strangely foreign faces so still, so lifeless, a sense of devastation swept through me. God, why had this happened? Who did this?

For a few minutes I couldn't even see them through the sheen of tears clouding my eyes. I leaned my hands on the edge of Danny's casket and drew in several deep, heaving breaths until I could get my emotions under control. When I opened my eyes again I gazed down on my little brother's inert form.

It felt like a knife pierced my heart.

I swear to God, brother. I promise I'll find out who did this to you. They're not going to get away with it. That's my solemn vow.

The visitation and the funeral service blurred together in my mind. There was a huge crowd of people in attendance. It seemed like I shook hundreds of hands, hugged countless necks, and bent to be kissed by dozens of women.

We went through the formalities, sang the appropriate songs, prayed the appropriate prayers. Then we caravanned to the cemetery. Rain spattered on the roof of the limousine, the tires whirring through the puddles the only sound as Grant, Tarina and I were driven to Haven's Gate.

A tent had been set up and we gathered under its protection for the final goodbye, the air hot and oppressive. As the minister droned on I became restless and let my gaze roam over the crowd. Was one of these people a killer? Had someone at this graveside murdered Danny and Eve?

When we arrived back at the house it was controlled chaos. Guests were pouring in, once again shaking my hand, slapping my back, offering condolences. I couldn't help but notice most of the mourners headed straight to the bar as soon as they finished speaking to me.

It almost seemed like a party atmosphere prevailed. Conversation flowed easily and laughter floated through the air. For a moment my fists clenched. How could these people who supposedly cared about Danny and Eve laugh? How can they make casual banter and tell each other jokes when my little brother and his wife are gone?

Anger knotted my jaw muscles. I wanted to scream at all of them to get the hell out. This wasn't a fucking party.

Then I caught sight of Jenna, Lily perched on her hip and DJ holding her hand. She looked so calm, so serene; she was like an oasis in the desert. Just looking at her soothed my soul. She glanced up and caught my eye, a sweet smile flickering across her face. It seemed her eyes were sending me a message, telling me she understood. Damn, when was the last time I felt like someone actually understood me?

I returned her smile and gave a slight lift to my glass, toasting her comforting presence. I saw Lily's thumb pop in her mouth and watched her curl her head into Jenna's neck, her big brown eyes blinking heavily. A moment later Jenna and the children left the room.

Jenna

I sat on the edge the glider rocker while DJ obediently sang the nursery rhyme. I had to grin as he sang faster and faster, eager to begin the hunt for Aunt Tarina.

DJ finished the requisite number of choruses then flung open the bedroom door.

"Ready or not. Here we come!"

DJ headed directly for the master bedroom and straight to the walk-in closet.

"Got ya!" he shouted when he tossed open the door.

"Oh, DJ, you found me. How did you know where to look?" Tarina looked at him as if she were amazed by his brilliance.

"Aw, Aunt Rina, you always hide here." DJ shrugged his little shoulders and Tarina and I both grinned. "Okay, now it's my turn. You coming, Jenna?"

"You bet I am. Lead the way, boss."

DJ grabbed my hand and pulled me down the hall.

"Hurry, Jenna, hurry. We need to make it all the way to Daddy's office. We'll hide in the closet there."

"There's a good hiding spot in here," he promised as he led me into the darkened room. He pulled me towards the slatted wooden doors and pushed his way into the closet, hunkering down behind a stack of boxes. I sank down beside him.

"Okay, now we wait."

It seemed only a few moments had passed when I heard the office door click open. Wow. How had she found us so fast? I leaned forward to peer through the louvres and see how close she was.

Holy crap. That wasn't Tarina. It was Joe Fielder. What the hell was he doing in Danny's office?

I turned to DJ and placed my finger on my lips, warning him to be quiet. I peeked out the louvers again and spotted Joe rifling through the desk. He thoroughly inspected every cranny before slamming the last drawer shut. With a disgusted look on his face he rose and scanned the room, his glance landing on the filing cabinet. He had just pulled the top drawer open when the office door opened once again.

Joe whirled at the sound of the latch, a look of panic on his face. He sagged with relief when he realized it was Tarina.

"Joe, what are you doing in here?" I watched through the crack as she moved towards him.

"You know what I'm doing, baby. I'm looking for evidence Danny had against me. Against us." He moved closer and wrapped his beefy arms around her waist. "I know he was on to us. I found the bug on the phone at the restaurant. He knew about the money laundering. I've got to find that recording. Help me look for it."

"God damn it, Joe. You killed my sister. Why should I help you do anything?"

"She was a wild card. You knew this was a risky operation when you got in on it. Better her dead than us in prison, right? Besides, you love me."

A tormented expression flashed across Tarina's face before she collapsed against Joe's chest,

"And honey, you've got to understand what I have to do next. You're not going to like it but it's to protect us. Because if I get fingered, you're going down with me and, babe, with that black hair you'll look like hell in prison orange.

Chapter 17: Trouble Is Coming

Jenna

"What are you saying?" Tarina drew back in horror. "You're not going to hurt my nephew?"

"Got to do it, babe." Joe stroked one finger down her cheek. "Can't take any chances. We've got a big future in front of us. Plenty of money. A tropical island. That's if there aren't any roadblocks. And unfortunately, DJ is a big fucking obstruction. He's the only possible person who could bring us down."

"No, Joe. You can't do it. He's just a baby." Tarina grabbed his shirt in two hands and jerked him close to her. "He doesn't know. He would have already told somebody if he recognized you. For God's sake, he's just three years old. He wouldn't keep that a secret."

"God damn it, Tarina. He's a loose end and loose ends can't be tolerated. Now you listen to me. You will help me find the boy and get him outside. If you don't" he paused, staring into her eyes, "you will go to prison with me. I'll tell them all about your role in the money laundering scheme and how you helped plot Danny and Eve's murder."

"But I didn't."

"You willing to bet your freedom on that?" he glared at her, his face a mask of cold insolence.

Tarina flung her chin up in defiance. "I am. I can't let you harm my nephew. This has gone too far."

"So, you think you're going to stop me?"

Tarina glared right back at him.

"I don't think so," Joe replied just before raising his arm and socking Tarina right in the temple. She crumpled to the ground like a discarded newspaper.

Holy crap. My heart thundered so hard I was sure Joe Fielder could hear its pounding. He wanted to kill DJ.

Over my dead body.

Of course, I'm sure Joe could easily arrange that if he found us hiding here.

I froze in position for a long moment, unsure of what to do. What if Joe decided to search this closet? We'd be sitting ducks.

Without saying a word, I drew DJ to me and silently scrounged farther back into the depths of the large closet. I pulled the tails of a wool tweed trench coat in front of us and held my breath while offering up a prayer that DJ would stay quiet.

"Don't make a sound." I barely breathed the words in his ear.

I could hear shuffling noises in the office and knew Joe was still out there. Dear God, it sounded like he was right outside the door.

My heart stopped beating when I heard the closet door slide open followed by a couple thumps that must have been Tarina's unconscious form being shoved into the dark space.

"I'll be back for you later," he growled before shutting the door.

Oh my God. By some miracle he hadn't seen DJ and me crouching in the shadows beneath the heavy coat. My heart slowly began to beat again.

I didn't move for a long moment, waiting, listening. I heard the outer door close but still froze in position. DJ's squirming brought me back to life. I had to get him out of here, get to Jake. The thought kept reverberating in my head. Find Jake.

It wasn't easy maneuvering over Tarina's still form. I paused to make sure she was still breathing then reached to help Jake climb over his aunt.

"Aunt Rina fall down now," he whimpered, wrapping his arms tight around my neck.

"She'll be okay, DJ. But we've got to hurry and find help for her." I didn't put him down as I headed for the office door. "We're going to find Uncle Jake."

Lord knows I didn't want to open that door and step into that hallway. I wished I had my cell phone with me and could just call Jake. Danny hadn't had a landline installed in this room so phoning for help was not an option. Well, I couldn't just stand here until Joe returned. Drawing in a deep breath and hitching DJ higher on my hip I reached to open the door just enough to peek out. The coast looked clear so I stepped into the hall.

Now we just had to make it to the family room...

That's when it happened. The door to DJ's bedroom opened and Joe Fielder stepped into the hallway.

The surprise halted me in my tracks. My mouth went dry, my heart racing. My arms tightened around DJ's small body pressed against mine.

"DJ, hi there. I've been looking for you." Joe flashed a friendly grin. "I saved you a piece of your favorite peanut butter pie." Joe looked at me and added. "DJ loves my peanut butter pie. Don't you, bud?"

"That's great. We'll get some in just a minute." I attempted to walk on but Joe stepped in front of me.

"You want your pie now don't you, buddy?"

"I do. But we gotta find Uncle Jake. Aunt Rina needs help. She fall down."

I couldn't stop him in time. The words tumbled out of his innocent mouth before I could slap my hand over it.

Joe's bushy eyebrows slashed down over stony eyes, his mouth thinning to a straight line.

"How do you know that, DJ?"

"We saw her in Daddy's office. She fall down."

Every word out of the little boy's mouth was like a nail in our coffins. I did my best to cough and cover up his voice but I knew it didn't work.

"Let's go, DJ." I moved to pass Joe's burly shape, trying to brazen our way out of there, but it didn't have a snowball's chance in hell of working. Out of nowhere a pistol appeared in Joe's hand aimed right at DJ's head.

"I think we better take a walk."

Chapter 18: Evil Comes Out

Jake

It seemed like a long time since I'd seen Jenna. I scanned the room looking for her and the kids but they weren't here. I wanted to talk to her, to relieve her from some of the responsibility of guarding DJ. Besides, I could use some of her calming influence myself. Tension racked my body, an uneasy feeling saturating me.

I managed to work my way towards Lily's room. The baby had looked so sleepy when I'd seen her last I was sure Jenna had gone to put her down for a nap. I popped my head into the room and saw my niece snuggled in her crib, bottom sticking straight up in the air. But no Jenna or DJ.

I moved on down the hall, glancing in DJ's room, the laundry room and Jenna's quarters. The only other room down here was Danny's office. Why they would be in there I had no idea but I'd look anyway just to be sure.

I opened the door and flicked on the light. I didn't see anybody but a strange thumping sound caught my attention. What the hell? It sounded like it was coming from the closet. I strode across the room and pulled open the slatted doors.

The sight of Tarina trussed up on the floor, hands and ankles bound with duct tape, her mouth covered in the sticky silver substance made my heart sink.

I knelt down at her side and ripped the duct tape off her mouth.

"What happened?" She looked dazed and I gave her shoulders a shake. "Tell me what happened. Who did this?"

"Joe. It's Joe and he's after DJ. He's going to kill him." She sobbed as she whispered the words. "Oh, God, Jake. Stop him."

Ice formed around my heart as her words slowly sank in. Joe. God, I had to find DJ and Jenna.

Now.

A roaring sound swelled in my ears as I stripped tape away from Tarina's wrists and ankles and helped her climb unsteadily to her feet.

"Can you walk? Are you okay?" I held on to her arms while she fought for balance before nodding.

"Then go find Grant or Detective Wayne and tell them what's happening. I'm going to look for DJ and Jenna."

She stumbled out of the room and I stood still for a moment trying to think. Think like a criminal. If I was Joe and I had DJ and Jenna, what would I do next? Where would I go? You can't just parade two hostages through a crowd of people like the one here tonight. He'd have to sneak off with them.

The door in Jenna's room led right to the deck and down to the lower level. From there it was an easy walk to the driveway. I was willing to bet that's how he'd take them out.

It seemed like it took me forever to get back to Jenna's room, my legs leaden with fear. When I got there the patio doors were standing open, curtains billowing in the wind and rain splattering across the hardwood floors.

Damn! They'd already been here and were gone.

Jenna

"Move it. Get out there now." Joe snapped the order, waving his gun in my face. I turned knowing if I carried DJ out that door we were probably goners. Behind me, Joe kept mumbling and talking to himself.

"God damn it, this just keeps getting worse. Now I not only have to take care of the kid, I have to take care of the babysitter. Son of a bitch."

The prod of the gun in my back urged me forward. The wind slapped me hard, smacking me with stinging raindrops as we emerged onto the deck. I tried to cover DJ as best I could.

"Fucking Tarina, too. I got to get her. Can't trust her anymore."

His tirade continued behind me as I made my way across the wet wood of the deck. It wasn't easy to maneuver in this weather with my heels on and DJ in my arms. I stepped carefully, listening to Joe ranting on. He sounded like he was losing it.

"Gotta call Reno. Gotta get the hell out of town. Go to Canada, catch a plane. Gotta go now."

I risked a glance over my shoulder at him. His eyes darted back and forth like he was trying to see in all directions at once and he was waving his hands around. This was not a man in his right mind.

We came to the stairs and I stopped. It wouldn't be an easy descent in the rain carrying DJ clinging fiercely to my neck.

"Don't stop now, woman. Get on down there."

"It's slick. I might fall."

"Get down those stairs or I'll kick you down them."

All righty then. I had no doubt he'd follow through on that threat so I turned back towards the staircase and took one hand off DJ so I could grip the handrail. The wind had ripped the pins from my hair and the thick curls flew in front of my eyes, minimizing my vision. I tried to take the steps as slowly as possible both for safety's sake and to buy a tiny bit more time. That worked until we were about four steps from the bottom.

"Move it!" Joe barked and accompanied the command with the shove of a firm palm in the middle of my back.

He hit me hard enough the momentum sent my feet sliding across the wet wood and one flew off the edge of the tread. I tumbled down the next step, clinging to DJ for dear life but we both went crashing and bouncing down the rest of the stairs. I didn't even recognize the scream ringing through the night as my own.

I did my best to twist and keep DJ on my body instead of landing on top of him but by the time we came to the bottom I lost my grip on him and he tipped out of my arms and launched onto the grass. I landed on the stone pavers at the bottom of the staircase, my hand twisted beneath me at an awkward angle.

Blinding pain shot through my arm and my stomach rolled. For a minute I couldn't see anything but a haze of red, then black. I drew in a sharp breath, then another one, and fought back the urge to pass out. I didn't dare. I had to take care of DJ.

I heard him crying and forced myself to set up, battling off a wave of dizziness. I crawled towards him, my knees scraping along the stones before I reached the soggy grass.

"DJ, buddy, I'm right here. Are you okay, little man?"

Joe came stomping up behind me just as I reached DJ.

"What the hell, you clumsy bitch. Get that kid and get moving. Head towards the van. Don't be pulling any more crazy stunts like that or I'll shoot you right here."

For a long moment I didn't move except to use my uninjured arm to draw DJ close to my body. I sat there hunched over the sobbing little boy, the rain beating down on us, thunder grumbling angrily in the background. Despite the heat of the evening I shivered uncontrollably. I turned and raised my head to look at the madman standing there with his gun pointed at us.

"You know what, Joe." Fatigue and pain edged my voice. "I guess that's just what you're going to have to do because we're not going anywhere with you."

Chapter 19: Stepping Up

Jake

Darkness had fallen early this evening, thick banks of clouds blocking any lingering sunlight. When I stepped onto the deck rain walloped me in the face and the wind blasted me with its force.

I'd always claimed to have balls of steel but right now I felt a fear like I had never known before. DJ and Jenna. I hadn't prayed for a long time but now that's all I could do.

"Please, please, please, God." The words reverberated over and over again in my head. "Please help me help them."

I moved a few steps forward then paused to listen. At first all I heard was the howling of the wind, raindrops spattering on the deck, and angry waves beating at the nearby shore.

Then I heard a scream echoed by DJ's hysterical cries. I rushed forward but froze at the top of the stairs. My blood ran cold at the sight in front of me.

Joe Fielder stood at the foot of the stairs, his back to me, facing the yard. Jenna knelt there in a puddle, soaking wet hair plastered against her head, muddy splotches on her dress. DJ curled up against her, his little face pale, hands clenched in Jenna's skirt.

That's when I felt the fear leave me and a cold determination take over. This was the bastard who had killed Danny and Eve. He wasn't going to take DJ and Jenna, too. For God's sake, DJ was a baby. He had his whole life ahead of him.

And Jenna. Lord, I had just found her. She'd come into my life like an unexpected jackpot. I didn't know why she had changed my entire attitude towards women, but she had managed to do it in just a few short days. Somehow I knew I had spent all this time going though women like some people go through breath mints looking for this one special lady. My queen of hearts. I couldn't lose her now. Or DJ either. It was time for the killing to stop.

I'd gambled millions of dollars at the poker tables. Played in high stakes games around the world. But this was the biggest gamble I'd taken yet. It was all in, winner take everything...and the loser dies.

Jenna

I raised my chin defiantly and glared at Joe. I still had trouble believing that Joe Fielder, Danny's right hand man, was the killer. And now he was going to kill me and DJ. God, he could take me, but help me find a way to get DJ out of here.

Getting in that van was not an option.

"Just tell me this, Joe. Why? You had a good job, a boss who respected you, trusted you, who paid you well. Why did you get involved in this shit and blow all that?" I wanted to keep him talking, praying for an opportunity to throw dirt in his eyes or something. Anything that would get us out of this mess.

"Oh, yeah. Great job. I did all the work and Danny got all the profits. He lived the high life and I settled for scraps. I wanted more, needed more."

"Well, since you're so damned and determined to kill me, you might as well tell me the whole story before I die so I know why this happened. How'd you get into money laundering?"

Joe shrugged and started talking.

"It was Reno's idea. He was heavy into selling heroin, got hooked up with a big connection. Did a lot of business out of DeMarco's. Tarina was one of his best customers. I needed money to keep her fixed up. I had the restaurant with thousands of dollars passing through it a night. It was a match made in heaven." The sound of his evil chuckle sent icebergs skimming through my veins.

"Fucking Tarina." He started to rant again. "Fucking bitch turning against me. I did all this for her. She wanted her drugs, she wanted money, she wanted to live like a fucking millionaire. Like her high class sister. I had to do it to keep her."

Just beyond the side of Joe's head my eyes caught sight of a movement. Was somebody there? I talked faster, louder, trying to keep Joe's attention riveted on me.

So you're telling me you were pussy whipped." I put as much scorn and derision in my tone as I could. "And look where it got you. Now you're on the run. Your life is ruined. And you're gonna get caught, Joe. You're gonna get caught and you're going to fry. Besides the money laundering charges you're going down for murder, multiple times."

Now I could tell it was Jake poised at the top of the stairs, stealthily moving forward. He was on the first step, the second. Just a little closer...

"Shut up, bitch. I'm not pussy whipped." He shouted indignantly and took a step forward, thrusting the gun towards my face.

I tossed my head back and laughed.

"You're so pussy whipped I bet you can't even get it up for another woman. Bet you can't get a hard on unless Tarina sucks you first." Damn, I hated the scummy words coming from my mouth, hated that DJ was hearing me talk like that. But I had to keep his attention. Had to provide cover for the sound of Jake creeping ever closer. He was just three stairs away now.

Joe raked his cold gaze across me, spending extra time on my heaving breasts and my upper thighs exposed by the skirt that had been pulled nearly to my hips by DJ's gnawing fingers.

"Oh, I can get it up all right. I'm gonna show you just how hard my dick can get." His hand reached down and cupped his crotch and shook it obscenely. "But first I'm going to kill that kid."

"No." The word burst from my throat and I threw myself over DJ, covering him with my body.

The last thing I saw before burying my head in the grass was Jake taking a flying leap and landing heavily on Joe's back.

I scrambled off the top of DJ and stood him on his feet.

"Run, DJ. Run into the house and yell for help."

For a minute I didn't think he was going to move but then he turned and his little legs began churning as he dashed up the stairs. Desperately I turned back to the fight between Jake and Joe.

Joe tumbled forward, the gun flying from his hand. Jake straddled his broad body and grabbed his ears, pounding his face into the ground.

Somehow Joe managed to twist away from Jake's grip and flip over. They both staggered to their feet and he drove one hammy fist directly into Jake's balls and Jake doubled over from the intense pain. Then Joe slammed a fist into Jake's jaw, sending him reeling backwards.

Jake recovered from Joe's last punch and threw a left into the shorter man's belly and Joe retaliated with a right hook, snapping Jake's head back.

God, I had to help him. If he lost this fight Joe would kill him...and me and DJ as well.

I glanced desperately around for a weapon. Anything I could hit him with.

And that's when I saw the gun lying just a few feet away.

I lunged for it and picked it up. I'd never shot a gun before but I was pretty sure how it worked. I hoisted it up and pointed it towards the battling men, cocking the hammer back, my wrist screaming in pain at the motion. Damn, what if I fired and missed Joe and hit Jake? My hands shook with tension. The tip of the pistol dipped and swayed as I tried to focus on Joe's bear-like body.

And then a gunshot shattered the air.

Chapter 20: Taking Care Of Business

Jake

I crept steadily downward, never taking my gaze off my prey. I heard Jenna's bold words, heard her desperately trying to cover the sound of my approach. Brave, stupid little fool. She was going to get herself shot if I didn't play this hand perfectly.

For just a moment I allowed myself to look at her. Her gaze met mine and I knew at that second that she trusted me completely. Her and DJ's lives were in my hands and she was betting on me. I couldn't let her down.

I stopped on the third step from the bottom, thankful the sound of my approach had been drowned out by the gusting wind and pounding waves teamed with Jenna's shouts. Drawing in a deep breath I tensed then sprang, flying through the air and landing square on top of Joe Fielder's back. The gun sailed out of his hand and landed in a puddle several feet away.

My hands slid across his bald head. There wasn't any hair to grab so I latched onto his ears and started pounding his face in the ground. Rage poured through me and all I wanted to do was pulverize him.

I don't know how he managed to flip me over and climb to his feet. I staggered up but when his fist slammed into my balls all the air whooshed out of my lungs and I couldn't breathe. His next punch to my jaw sent me staggering backwards, stunned.

Now I was fighting for my life as well. The only sound I heard was a roaring in my ears, all I saw was Joe Fielder, his face contorted, blood running from his nose.

I hadn't fought for quite a while but I hadn't forgotten how. All my military training, my time on the streets in the hoods of Chicago came back to me. I made a quick feint right then attacked from the left.

I was taller than Joe but he was built like a bull. He swayed on his feet but fought back, landing a good hard blow to my eye. I grabbed his shirt and drew back to aim a fist at his nose.

Before I could land the punch the sound of a gunshot reverberated through the air.

Jenna

Stunned, I stared at the gun in my hand. I hadn't pulled the trigger, had I?

My gaze flew to Jake and Joe. Jake held Joe up by his shirt as Joe's knees buckled. Blood spread from the wound in his shattered hip.

"Let him go, Jake." Detective Wayne's voice carried over the noise of the storm. "He's done. It's over."

Then I saw the police officer step into sight on the deck above us, his gun still aimed at Joe Fielder.

For a long moment Jake didn't move. Then he slowly released his grip on Joe and pushed him backwards, watching the man crumple at his feet. Jake stood over him, gasping for breath, battered and bloody.

To me he looked like an avenging hero, his wounds medals of honor. Then he turned and our gazes locked, a silent message traveling between us. I don't know who moved first but an instant later we were in each other's arms, hugging fiercely.

"Oh, God, Jake, oh God." I kept repeating the words as I clung to him, holding on like I would never let him go.

"Jenna, honey, are you all right?" He ran his hands over me as if searching for injuries and when he came to my wrist I cringed with pain.

"I'll be okay. But look at you. Jake, you're bleeding." I ran my thumb across his chin to wipe away the red liquid flowing there. His eye was already swelling shut.

We stood, clinging to each other as the rain pounded over us until suddenly we were surrounded by people. Grant ran up first then several cops and many of the guests swarmed around us.

I pulled back out of Jake's arms, searching for DJ.

Grant realized what I was looking for and told me DJ was inside with his Aunt Tarina.

"Jake, I want to see him. I have to see DJ."

"We'll go find him, babe." He wrapped his arm around my waist and I allowed myself to lean against him. God, it was over. It was all over.

A few minutes later we were inside. Jake held DJ in his arms, cuddling him close. The little boy seemed recovered from the worst of his scare and now was excitedly describing the whole incident to his uncle.

I didn't realize how cold I was until someone wrapped a warm blanket around my shoulders. I was drenched, my hair clinging to my neck and shoulders. My wet dress gripped my body, caked with mud. It would never be the same again.

Yet this still felt like one of the happiest moments in my life. DJ's dirty face was animated and glowing as he told his uncle all about the night's events. Jake and I looked at each other, sharing the moment, treasuring this lively child. Thank God he was still with us.

And then we were separated, paramedics coming to inspect our injuries, Detective Wayne barking questions. As I was poked and prodded and interrogated all at once I watched as Tarina was led away in handcuffs. Though she had played an instrumental part in saving our lives, Eve's sister had confessed to money laundering and lying about the alibi she'd provided for Joe the night of the murders. She'd have to deal with those infractions in court.

As much as I objected the paramedics insisted on carting me off to the hospital to have my wrist x-rayed. Jake protested even louder than I did but we ended up sharing an ambulance ride to the emergency room. I fussed about leaving the kids but Grant insisted he was perfectly capable of caring for two small children.

Detective Wayne drove us home from the hospital. Jake and I both climbed into the back seat and let the man play chauffer. I had a new neon pink cast on my wrist and Jake sported a dozen stitches on his jaw where Joe's ring had sliced into his skin.

The cop tried to interrogate us while he drove but Jake just looked at him and told him to shut up. Enough was enough.

Both of us were crashing from an adrenaline high, the trauma of tonight's events setting in. I laid my head on Jake's shoulder and he rested his arm behind my neck. For a long time, the only sounds were the shushing of the windshield wipers and the tires skimming across the rain drenched streets.

My wrist throbbed and hammers pounded in my skull but the worst pain of all was the one in my heart. God help me, I'd gone and fallen in love with the Playboy.

Chapter 21: Much Needed Rest

Jake

When Wayne started hammering away with questions again as soon as we got in his car I looked at Jenna's pale face and told him to shut up. We'd been through enough tonight. He could wait until morning for any more answers. I felt Jenna's shoulders sag with relief.

I closed my eyes for a moment and immediately flashed back to the terrifying sight of Jenna and DJ kneeling at the feet of Joe Fielder, his gun aimed right at them. DJ so small, his face smeared with mud, grass clinging to his sodden clothes. Jenna, so brave, her chin thrust up in defiance, her arms wrapped protectively around my nephew. The fear at that moment nearly choked me, cutting off my breath but I forced myself to move. I had to take this maniac down before he killed them.

When I heard that gunshot I froze. My heart stopped beating until I realized it was Joe that was hit, his weight dragging at my hand clutching his shirt. When Wayne ordered me to let him go I did it gladly. Of course I may have given him a little extra shove to make sure he landed firmly on the ground.

I couldn't get to Jenna fast enough. I held her trembling body tight, like I would never let her go.

And it was at that moment I realized I didn't want to ever let her go. I couldn't let her go. The thought of going back to my old way of life, floating from woman to woman, somehow felt so wrong. The appeal of all those other women had magically evaporated. There was only one woman I wanted now.

The problem was...how was I going to convince Jenna of that? I'd never been in this position before, never wanted to persuade a woman to be mine. Oh, I had a lot of practice making women go away. I'd never met one I wanted to be with exclusively. How did a guy with my reputation go about making a woman like Jenna believe she was all the woman he needed?

Wayne pulled up in front of the house and started to turn off the engine and get out of the car.

"No you don't." Cop or no cop, he wasn't coming in with us. We needed to rest and recuperate. And I needed time to think. "Say good night, detective. We'll talk to you tomorrow."

I shoved open the car door and stepped out then turned to take Jenna's uninjured hand and help her exit. We stood there together, arms around each other's waist, until the big sedan pulled away.

The rain had stopped, stars starting to sparkle across the night sky as the clouds scudded off to the east. The air was rich with that unique scent that you only smelled right after a storm. The earlier roar of the waves had softened to a gentle whooshing.

"Jenna." I turned to face her, my hand lifting to cup her cheek. She stared up at me with those indigo eyes and I tried my best to read what she was thinking. Then the urge to kiss her overwhelmed me and I lowered my head to gently taste her lips.

"Hey, you're back." Grant's voice imploded the moment. Jenna jerked back, startled, as Grant stepped off the porch and strode towards us. "Wow. What a night, huh? By the way, you two are a mess. Come on in the house."

For a moment I fought an urge to throttle Grant for interrupting but then I took a closer look at Jenna. Wet curls framed her pale face, the scattering of freckles across the bridge of her slender nose standing out like gold flakes on ivory wax. She needed dry clothes, a hot drink, and rest.

And I needed her.

Jenna

When Jake leaned down to kiss me my knees trembled. If it hadn't been for Grant's unexpected appearance I know I would have thrown myself into Jake's arms and clung to him like a burr. I should be grateful Grant had stopped me from making another big mistake.

"You don't have to tell me twice." I turned and headed into the house. "Are the kids okay?"

"They're fine, both sound asleep."

"Great. Okay, guys, I'm going to take a hot bath."

"When you're done, come back and I'll have Irish coffee waiting for you." Grant called after my retreating back.

I ran a tubful of steaming hot water and added my favorite orange blossom bath oil. It was awkward keeping my cast dry but the warm water soothed my aching muscles and calmed the thumping in my head. By the time I was finished, dried my hair, and dressed in a pair of soft knit leggings and a long T-shirt the thought of Irish coffee was appealing but I didn't really want to see Jake again tonight.

Instead I slipped down the hall to check on the kids. DJ had kicked off his blankets and I pulled them back over him, whispering a prayer of thankfulness that he was safe and sound. Then I tiptoed into Lily's room and watched her sleep, her thumb stuck in between her rosebud lips, her butt protruding in the air.

"They're safe, Jenna. We're all safe now."

I spun around to face Jake holding two coffee mugs in his hands.

"Thank God...and you...for that."

"And you," he added, handing her a cup. "It was you that kept DJ safe until I got there."

I couldn't look him in the eye, instead taking a long sip of the Irish coffee.

"It was my fault we got in that position," I confessed. "I should have never agreed to let him play hide and go seek. I should have told Tarina no."

Jake took my elbow and led me into the hall so we wouldn't wake Lily then gave me a stern look.

"I don't want to hear you talk like that, Jenna. None of this is your fault. It's all Joe and Tarina's fault. This whole ugly mess. You, pretty lady, are a heroine."

His words soothed my soul. I felt so guilty for getting DJ into danger.

"Come on out on the deck with me. Grant's gone to bed and we can enjoy some quiet time after all this craziness."

I knew I shouldn't go. Being alone with Jake was only begging for heartache. The logical part of me blared a warning but a bigger part of me couldn't resist the lure of this man. He was like a magnet pulling me to him.

I followed Jake outside and we sat together in a teak swing that swayed gently as we took our places. For a long moment we simply sat there, sipping our coffee and breathing in the sweet night air. Finally, I spoke.

"I can't believe this nightmare is over."

"Thank God. Jenna, I know I said we'd have to go to Vegas if this wasn't solved by today. Now that's not the case."

"I understand. But you need to go back anyway, right?" I dreaded his answer. I knew that's where his life was. It had been put on hold long enough.

"No, I don't have to get back right away. There will still be plenty of loose ends to wrap up around here. But I was wondering..."

He paused, almost like he was afraid to continue.

"Wondering?" I encouraged him to go on.

"How would you like it if we went there just for a vacation? You, me, and the kids? You'd be surprised just how family friendly Vegas really is." He reached out and pulled my hand into his own. "And I could hire a top notch babysitter so we could see some shows and enjoy the nightlife. It really is a great city and we could spend some time together. Get to know each other better."

His words took me by surprise. I know he needs me because of the kids but he sounded like he really wanted me to there, to let him take me places, be seen out and about with me. Like maybe I wasn't just the nanny. Almost like…a girlfriend.

"Aren't you afraid that would damage your reputation? I mean, how would it look for the Playboy to be seen out with the same woman more than once or twice?"

He drew my hand to his lips and kissed my fingers, looking directly in my eyes.

"If that woman is you, it will only enhance my reputation. Any man would be proud to have you on his arm."

I dropped my gaze in an attempt to break the trance this man cast on me. For a moment old insecurities popped up. I wasn't stylish or beautiful. I was a country girl who wouldn't fit in with the class of people Jake hung out with. Billionaires, celebrities, high rollers. I didn't even have the right clothes to wear.

"Hey, look at me." His voice was soft, compelling. Slowly I lifted my gaze back to his.

"You are the most beautiful woman I know. You're sexy as hell. Your body is so lush, so feminine. You've got the face of an angel. But you know what really makes you so rare and special?" He paused and gave me a gaze so intense it sent shock waves vibrating through me. "You have a natural beauty that shines from within. You care about others more than you do yourself. Do you know how rare a trait that is?"

He sounded sincere, his thumb rubbing across the top of my hand with a sensuous rhythm. But fear still chilled my blood. Jake was use to seducing women and tossing them away. This was a dangerous man and my heart was at risk. Was I willing to gamble on love with the Playboy?

Chapter 22: The Next Fix

Jake

I had a burning desire to make love to Jenna, but I knew this wasn't the time or the place. Jenna had been through hell tonight. She was hurt, shocked, and exhausted. I had no right to look at her with hungry eyes, an insatiable craving burning in me. She needed rest, needed time, needed to think. And so did I.

"Just think about it, Jenna. We'll talk more tomorrow."

One of the hardest things I've ever done is lean over and give Jenna a gentle peck on her forehead and tell her goodnight. I was not going to take advantage of her vulnerable state, no matter how badly I wanted her.

Her response was barely a whisper and I fought the urge to pull her back as she walked away. Instead I sat there on that glider on the deck, watching the waves roll to shore, pictures of Jenna drifting through my mind. Jenna, cuddling with Lily, blowing raspberries on the baby's cheek. Jenna soothing DJ in the middle of the night. Jenna, glowing in the aftermath of lovemaking, eyes dreamy, breasts heaving.

I wanted her more than anything I've ever desired. I could buy anything material I wanted. Yachts, palaces, gold mines. Hell, I knew a lot of women who were available for the right price.

But not Jenna.

Jenna couldn't be bought.

So if money wouldn't work, what did I have to offer her?

Only my heart.

Jenna

When I went to my room fatigue overwhelmed me and I thought I would fall asleep as soon as I lay down but it didn't happen. Pictures of the events of the evening flashed through my mind. My life had come so close to ending tonight an awareness of just how short life could be saturated me. It could terminate in an instant. Would I be satisfied if it ended without taking a chance on Jake? If I never experienced that soul shattering experience of making love with Jake again could I die happy? Something told me that would never be possible.

I knew Jake's request for me to go on vacation with him and the kids was more than just an appeal from an employer to an employee. The expression on his handsome face had made that perfectly clear. I didn't need to delude myself into thinking it was less than it was. I knew if I took him up on his suggestion I would wind up in bed with him again.

I held a losing hand, no doubt about it. Jake wasn't a man easily tamed. How could I believe I was enough woman to satisfy the Playboy permanently?

Maybe it couldn't be permanently.

Maybe it could just be for now.

Was I willing to take that gamble?

The yearning in my soul answered that question.

I wanted Jake DeMarco and I wanted him now. Despite the throbbing in my broken wrist, the fear in my heart, I didn't want to wait. Before I could lose my courage I got out of bed and headed down the hall.

When I came to the door of Jake's room I hesitated, my fist raised to knock. Once I rapped, there would be no going back.

With a quick intake of breath, I tapped on the door.

Jake

I'd spent the last 15 minutes pacing across my bedroom floor. Too pent up to sleep, I tried to walk off the agitation building inside me. Part of it was created by the drama of today, the rest due to my hunger for Jenna. I wanted nothing more than to march down that hall and sweep her in my arms, kiss her all over and convince her to stay with me.

When the knock sounded at my door I froze. If that was Grant, I was going to kill him. But if it was Jenna...my dick throbbed at the thought of her.

My heart jackhammered when I saw her in the doorway.

"I thought about it." She looked up shyly at me from beneath those long thick lashes. "I'd love to go on vacation with you."

I didn't say a word just pulled her into the room and wrapped my arms around her. I knew she wasn't just saying yes to a trip to Las Vegas. This was her way of telling me she was willing to take a chance on our relationship. Damn, that word sounded foreign. I'd never had one of those before.

But I was damn sure willing to give it a try.

My lips zeroed in on hers, trying to tell her without words how much she affected me, how she had turned my world around. All that mattered were her and the children. My only goal now was to make them happy.

Starting right now.

"Jenna, you know I want you. I want you with every breath that I take; every beat of my heart." I raised my mouth just long enough to whisper the words before recapturing her honeyed lips. "But what about your arm? I don't want to hurt you."

"Nothing could hurt me more right now than going without you."

"I promise I'll be gentle."

"I trust you, Jake."

Her soft words brought a golf ball sized lump to my throat. I vowed then and there I would do everything possible to deserve that trust. She wrapped her arms around my neck, the cast resting against my shoulders. I pulled her closer, my lips traveling to her ear.

"I'm going to make you glad you do." My hands slid along her back and cupped her butt, pulling her against the rock hard erection in my pants. I picked her up and her legs wrapped around my waist and a groan rumbled through me. I walked purposefully towards the bed and collapsed on the mattress with her beneath me.

I didn't want to hurry this tonight. I planned on savoring every second with her, relishing each special moment. My lips trailed along her hairline, pressing tiny kisses across her forehead, skimming to her ear, my teeth nipping gently at the lobe. She smelled like orange blossoms and vanilla, the scent stirring my senses.

My hands explored every inch of her body, massaging, soothing, treasuring the feel of her silky skin. When I went to pull her top off I moved with utmost caution, not wanting to hurt her injured arm. Once she was free of that garment I was free to devour her. I allowed my gaze to feast on her generous breasts.

"So beautiful." I whispered the words as I bowed my head to suck her nipple into my mouth, my hand cupping the mound of flesh, my tongue sweeping across the extended bud. "So sweet."

Slowly I let my tongue trail down to her navel and dip inside it. I loved the way it made her squirm against me, her pelvis rising, soft moans of desire coming from her lips. I rose on my elbow and looked into her lust-glazed eyes, drinking in the site of her flushed face. Our eyes met and words weren't necessary. The emotion there was rare and new, piercing deep into my heart. I savored this fresh pleasure, these feelings of intimacy and soul sharing. Just through our gazes confessions were made, love declared.

I didn't look away as I skimmed her pants down and let my hand slide to the damp portal between her legs. She opened for me and my fingers slid across the moist tissue, exploring slowly, slipping gently across her budding clit. Her breathing grew faster, her moans turned to whimpers, and a look of pure bliss passed across her face.

Then my lips replaced my fingers. I slashed my tongue along that damp valley, grazing over the clit, flicking and tickling it until her hips were thrashing so hard I grabbed her butt and held her to me. I drank in her wetness like it was a fine wine. In the next moment when her orgasm exploded I didn't let up, the tip of my tongue teasing her entrance, lapping up her flowing juices.

I moved to shed my clothes and reach into the nightstand and retrieve a condom, rolling it quickly into place before returning to the nest between her legs. It took all my will power to move slowly, gradually easing into her heated canal. Just as slowly I retreated then moved steadily deeper. Stroke by stroke I tried to show her how much she meant to me, how different this action was with her than all those other women. For the first time in my life I wasn't just having sex. I was making love.

I felt my orgasm fighting for release but I wanted her to come again first. I reached between us and let my thumb roll across her clit and she cried out, stiffening as spasms racked through her, her pussy clenching fiercely around my dick.

I couldn't hold back any more. Her name wrenched from my lips as hot seed poured out, throbbing shudders rocketing through my body. I clutched her to me, unable to get her close enough, melding into her very being.

This wasn't just physical; it was life altering.

Chapter 23: The Biggest Gamble of Them All?

Jenna

I couldn't help it. Emotions overwhelmed me. So much had happened, so quickly. I couldn't stop the tears that ran down my face. I buried my face in Jake's shoulder and let them come.

"Oh, God, Jenna, baby. Did I hurt you? Is it your arm?" Jake's hands ran through my hair, stroking it back from my face before kissing my tear wet cheeks. "I'm sorry, honey. So sorry."

I had to struggle to get my breath before I could speak.

"No, no, it's not my arm. I don't know why I'm crying. I just can't help it."

Jake soothed me with nonsensical words and butterfly kisses, holding me close and letting me cry against him. His hands stroked my back and caressed my shoulders until I managed to stifle my tears.

"Jenna." He rose up and looked at me. "Are you afraid? Afraid of what's growing between us?"

I drew in a long shuddering breath before I nodded.

"I am, too," he confessed. "I've never felt like this before. Didn't know it was even possible to feel this way. But I'm not going to let fear keep me from betting on us. I learned a long time ago to trust my gut and now I've got to trust my heart. I'm a gambler. I don't go into a game thinking I'm going to lose. Gong all in on a hand is always scary but I do it when the risk is worth it. And I think we're worth the gamble. Are you with me?"

I locked gazes with him, looking deep, trying to see into his soul. I raised my hand and caressed his cheek, my thumb gently stroking his stitches. His eye was puffy and purple. Battle scars from today's trauma. I didn't see the Playboy there. I saw my hero, my love. Was I willing to bet on him?

"I'm in, Jake," I whispered. "I'm all in."

Epilogue

Jenna

It's hard to believe it's been nearly a year since Danny and Eve DeMarco were laid to rest. Today we'd been in the courtroom to hear the guilty verdict read against Joe Fielder. It didn't ease the loss of the young couple, but it did offer us some sense of closure. Reno Vasquez had also been convicted for his part in the money laundering scheme and Eve's sister pleaded guilty to some lesser counts. She'd be getting out of jail in a few weeks and Jake and I planned to offer her plenty of help to make a new start.

So much had happened in these past twelve months. We'd gone to Vegas and had a great time. Jake's penthouse was spectacular though we spent a couple days babyproofing the place. It hadn't been designed for toddlers. The kids loved it there and we spent a lot of time at the pool and visiting the many nearby parks. I even discovered most of Jake's friends were good people who accepted me into their group right away.

Jake was incredibly generous. He showered me with gifts and lavished me with love. We went to see Cirque de Soleil and a dozen other shows. He wasted no time in letting his cohorts know that he was no longer the Playboy, but was now a one-woman man. Sometimes it was still hard to believe I was that woman.

Las Vegas wasn't the only place we visited. We took the kids on a trip to Disney World. I don't know who had more fun, them or us.

We spent the majority of our time in Michigan City but it wasn't unusual for us to travel back to Vegas or to another city so Jake could play in the big poker tournaments or take care of business.

He hadn't forgotten his promise to investigate my parents' murder, either. It wasn't solved yet but he had Grant and his team working hard to discover the truth.

And I hadn't forgotten my determination to go to law school but I wasn't in any hurry now. I wanted to wait until the kids were both in school. DJ would be starting kindergarten in the fall and Lily would be heading to preschool. They were growing up too fast. I wanted to spend this time with them while they're little.

Tonight Jake and I were going to celebrate the end of the trial. It had been a grueling experience. We both had to testify and just looking at Joe brought back dark emotions. Reliving the nightmare tortured both of us. Now, except for the sentencing, it was over.

I sat at the vanity running a brush through my curls and stared at my reflection. I look different I decided. Being in love put a glow in my cheeks, added serenity to my face. Taking a gamble on Jake had been the smartest bet I'd ever made.

I stood and slipped on a violet silk dress that showed off my figure and enhanced the color of my eyes. Jake had seen it in a shop window and insisted I have it. I loved the feel of the sensuous fabric. He'd even bought me matching high heeled sandals.

I'd just finished fastening my opal and diamond pendant when I heard a small rap at the door followed by an abundance of giggles. I smiled as I opened the door and two curly black mops popped in.

"Aunt Jenna, Uncle Jake said to tell you to shake a tail feather." DJ clapped his hand over his mouth after delivering the message, his chocolate brown eyes gleaming with laughter.

"I told him you don't have feathers." Lily looked serious. "Do you, Jenna? Do you have a tail feather?"

I bent and dropped a kiss on her silky tresses.

"No, Lilybell, I don't have a tail feather. Uncle Jake was teasing. It's just a way of telling me to hurry up. I guess he's ready to go."

"Miss Frankie's here," DJ announced. "And Mr. Grant, too."

That was surprising news. I knew my friend Frankie the librarian was coming to stay with the kids tonight while Jake and I went out but I didn't know Grant was coming as well.

"Mr. Grant, too?"

"Yeah, come on." Each child grabbed one of my hands and pulled me towards the great room. I couldn't help laughing as I hurried to keep up with them.

My laughter changed to silent amazement as I walked into the spacious room. It had been transformed. Big red and white heart-shaped balloons floated everywhere and a white upholstered high back chair stood next to the fireplace filled with dozens of red roses. A trail of scarlet rose petals formed a path leading directly from the hall to the throne-like chair.

The sound of heralding trumpets sounded through the speakers and Grant stepped out of the shadows. Clad in a white silk shirt and slim fitting black pants that hugged his muscular thighs he strode towards me and bowed low before holding out his hand. Like a knight of old he led me formally to the chair then turned to face our audience of four.

"Ladies and gentleman, may I present...the Queen of Hearts. Her crown please."

Lily toddled forward holding a red heart pillow bearing a golden crown complete with scarlet hearts embedded around its surface. When she curtsied before holding the pillow out to me my heart melted.

"Let me help you put that on." Grant took the crown and placed it gently on my head, his gazed locked on mine. "My lady, will you please take your throne?"

Still awe struck I turned and sank into the velvet covered chair. What was going on? Jake had surprised me many times but this was beyond the unexpected.

I had no idea what he was up to until he sank on one knee before me and took my hand in his. I'd never seen such a serious look on his face.

"Jenna, a year ago you decided to take a gamble on me and I hope you believe its paid off. You've won my love, my devotion, and my heart. I can't imagine my home or my life without you in it. You are my queen of hearts."

He paused and I saw a suspicious wetness in his eyes as he pulled a tiny box from his pants pocket. He flipped it open to reveal a stunning heart shaped diamond ring. God, was this really happening?

"Jenna, I love you, DJ and Lily love you. Will you marry me and make it a full house?"

"Yeah, Jenna, marry him. Then you'll be our real aunt." DJ and Lily cheered and clapped.

I cast a look at Grant and Frankie, our best friends, then turned my gaze at those sweet children I'd come to love as my own. Finally, I turned back to face Jake, tears shimmering in my eyes. If one could die of happiness I was sure my time had come.

"Yes, Jake, yes, yes." I reached out and wrapped my arms around his shoulders pulling him close so I could rain dozens of kisses across his face. I was laughing and crying all at once. Then DJ and Lily ran forward and we were engulfed in happy hugs and sweet as sugar kisses.

Who would believe it? The reality of it still stunned me. The billionaire and the babysitter. Wow. God really does move in mysterious ways.

About The Author

Simone Carter is a passionate Romance Author. She initially started writing in her spare time after University, and 10 years later she's managed to turn it into a full time venture.

She loves to write promiscuous stories that feature strong, sassy women, in an array of different settings and scenarios.

Simone lives in Colorado with her husband and two children. When she's not creating steamy story lines, you can find her spending time with her family, hiking trails, or at home on her balcony with a book and a nice glass of wine.

You can download a FREE book from Simone "A Women's Prerogative" and join her exclusive mailing list. You'll receive notifications of huge discounts, FREE promotions, and hot, new release dates. Sign up to Simone's mailing list here:

http://hrdpub.com/simone-carter

Other titles by Simone Carter

If you enjoyed reading "*Clandestine, A Secret Affair*", you might want to check out her other titles:

Lesbian: Uncovering Charlee

Lesbian: Heaven Sent

Lesbian: Private Investigations

Ménage: Three Dollar Bill

Ménage: Good Things Come In Threes

Printed in Great Britain
by Amazon